Blunt Darts

A Great New Detective and A Highly Acclaimed New Author for Mystery Fans

"Mr. Healy writes so well that he tends to transcend the clichés. Indeed, if the ensuing Cuddy books turn out as successfully as this (the author has promised to continue the series), the popular Spenser is going to have some real competition. Cuddy . . . is quite a package . . . and there is a slam-bang sequence with a chilling conclusion. The plotting is impeccable, and everything comes together to make *Blunt Darts* one of the outstanding first mysteries of the year 1984."
—*New York Times Book Review*

"A welcome new Boston private eye . . . wise, well-paced, instructive, and fun. The characters possess more depth and intelligence than a season of television sleuths. Though I read *Blunt Darts* in one sitting, I found myself reading slowly, unable to put the book down, yet reluctant to get to the end."
—*Chicago Sun-Times*

"Impressive . . . hair-raising. . . . The tone of the book is terse and understated, and the first-person narration is laced with ironic observations. Healy has created a very realistic and likable character."
—*Publishers Weekly*

"It is hard to avoid comparisons with Robert Parker's immensely popular Spenser series. . . . But Healy's story is tighter than most of Parker's recent efforts, and there is a gut-wrenching twist at the conclusion that will make it easy for readers to remember and admire Healy and his hero."
—*Wilson Library Bulletin*

ABOUT THE AUTHOR

Jeremiah Healy is a graduate of Rutgers College and Harvard Law School. He served in the Military Police and practiced civil litigation with a Boston law firm. In 1978, Healy joined the faculty of New England School of Law, becoming a full professor in 1983. He and his wife, Bonnie Tisler, a buyer for Filene's, live in Boston and divide their vacations between Maine and the Caribbean. BLUNT DARTS is his first novel.

Blunt Darts

J. F. Healy

POPULAR LIBRARY

An Imprint of Warner Books, Inc.

A Warner Communications Company

To Bonnie, who is Beth

All the characters and events portrayed in this story are fictitious.

POPULAR LIBRARY EDITION

Popular Library® is a registered trademark of Warner Books, Inc.

This Popular Library Edition is published by arrangement with
Walker and Company, 720 Fifth Avenue, New York, N.Y. 10019

Cover art by Don Ivan Punchatz

Popular Library books are published by
Warner Books, Inc.
666 Fifth Avenue
New York, N.Y. 10103

W A Warner Communications Company

Printed in the United States of America

First Popular Library Printing: June, 1986

10 9 8 7 6 5 4 3 2 1

First

"NAME?"

"Cuddy, John Francis."

"Address?"

"74 Charles Street."

"In Boston?"

"In Boston."

"Social Security number?"

"040-93-7071."

"Date of birth?"

I told her.

She looked up at me, squeezed out a smile. "You look younger."

"It's a mark of my immaturity," I said. She made a sour face and returned to the form.

"Occupation?"

"Investigator."

"Previous employer?"

"Empire Insurance Company." I wondered whether Empire had to fill out a form that referred to me as "Previous Employee."

"Reason for leaving previous employment?"

"I have a letter." I took the letter from my inside coat pocket and handed it to her. Opening it and reading it slowed her down. I looked around the big, clattering room at the thirty or so other metal desks.

5

Each had a woman filling out a form and an applicant answering the same questions. Most of the applicants were men. I wondered why we applicants couldn't fill out at least the first few lines by ourselves.

The man seated at the desk next to me sneezed. Brittlely old and black, he looked as though he should have been applying for Social Security instead of unemployment. He wiped his nose with a clean handkerchief that had a hole in one corner. When he was finished he folded it so that the hole didn't show.

"Mr. Cuddy, if you'll pay attention to me, we'll finish this procedure much more quickly."

I turned my head to face her again. "That's all right," I said. "I've got time."

She fixed me with the sour look again and tapped her index finger on the paper before her. "This letter from your previous employer is beautifully drafted, Mr. Cuddy, probably by a company lawyer. It nicely provides every fact the regulations require. Accordingly, I have no choice but to recommend you for benefits. I must say, however, that seeing a man of your obvious abilities here instead of out in the world earning his way makes me sick."

"I didn't think you were looking too well. Would you like me to complete the rest of the form myself?"

"No!" she snapped. I thought I heard the man next to me stifle a chuckle. She and I operated as a much more efficient team after that.

"Education?"

"High School, then Holy Cross. One year of night law school."

"Military service?"

"Military Police, discharged a captain in nineteen-sixty-eight."

"Employer prior to Empire Insurance Company?"

"Just the army."

She looked up at me again. "Do you mean you worked for Empire since nineteen-sixty-eight?"

"Since nineteen-sixty-nine. I traveled around the country for a while after the service."

She shook her head, and we completed the rest of the form. I signed it and got a brochure explaining my benefits and rights. I also received a little chit that entitled me to stand in a slow-moving line ten or twelve people deep in front of a window like a bank teller's.

I had to hand it to Empire. They really knew how to deal with someone like me. After nearly eight years with them, I became head of claims investigation in Boston. It meant my own office, with a window. Beth and I were just this side of ecstasy. We'd married during my first year with Empire and had always lived in apartments in Back Bay, a quiet part of the city within walking distance of the office. With the promotion, we decided we could finally plunge for a three-bedroom condominium there. We moved in during the hottest week in July. Four months later, the doctor told us what Beth had inside her head.

The insurance covered eighty percent of the medical expenses, and a second mortgage on the condo covered most of the rest for the first nine months. I would have sold the place, but it was in both our names, and Beth refused to give it up until the beginning of the last month, when she finally admitted to herself (but never once to me) that she wouldn't be coming home. I sandwiched selling the place between trips to the office and the hospital. I turned most of our furniture over to an auctioneer and moved the rest into a small one-bedroom apartment on Charles Street at the foot of Beacon Hill.

Three weeks later, Joe Mirelli, the priest who'd

grown up with us in South Boston and married us there, helped me ease Beth into a small piece of ground on a gentle slope overlooking the harbor.

Two months to the day after Beth's funeral, the head of Boston claims walked into my office. I had my window open a crack, and I could hear Christmas carols carrying from some store's outside stereo speakers. He handed me an investigation report and told me to sign it. I read the report, which substantiated a five-figure jewel-theft claim from an affluent bedroom community just west of Boston, and looked up at him. "This may win this year's award for best short fiction, but I'm not going to sign it."

"Sign it."

"No."

"John, please—just sign it."

"Phil, nobody from this office ever investigated this claim."

"John, I've been told to tell you to sign it."

"Phil, you've also just been told that I'm not going to."

Phil took the report back and left my office.

The next day the head of claims investigation and the head of the claims division, both from home office, were outside my office with Phil when I arrived. It was a cold December day, but at 8:15 A.M., Phil already had patches of sweat in the armpits of his button-down shirt.

"Sign it," said Head of Claims.

"The investigation was never done," I replied.

"It was done by an independent outfit without your knowledge," said Head of Investigation.

"Fine. Let me talk to him, her, or it."

"That's not feasible," said Head of Claims.

"Then let him, her, or it sign the report."

Phil picked up the report and shook it at me. "Christ, John, will you please sign the goddamned thing?" He was squealing.

"No."

"Well," said Head of Claims as he plucked the report from Phil's hand and tamped it into his inside pocket, "that's certainly clear enough." Head of Claims walked out the door followed by Phil, who said, " 'Bye, John."

" 'Bye, John," mimicked Head of Investigation as he followed them out and closed the door.

Fifteen minutes later I called Tommy Kramer. He was a college classmate of mine and the best lawyer I knew who had no connection with the company. I explained what had happened. He said to wait and see what developed. I didn't have long to wait.

Two days later, Head of Boston Office called me into his office. His window was closed, but I imagine we were too high up to hear Christmas carols anyway.

He was in his early sixties and Ivy League. He came from a Pilgrim-tracing North Shore family, though by the time his generation arrived, the bloodline had run a bit thin. After a few minutes of uncomfortable small talk, he allowed as how my senior investigator, Mullen, was due for a promotion. He also allowed as how I'd gone about as far as I could with the company and should consider seeking "lateral-level" employment elsewhere, toward which I'd receive only the highest references. He had never heard of any five-figure claim or investigation report. When he added, jokingly, that I could, of course, be terminated in such a way as to qualify for unemployment compensation, I took him up on it. He was shocked and tried to talk me out of it, but I insisted. He reluctantly agreed to get the in-house attorney started on it.

When I got back to my office, I called Tommy Kramer again. I told him what I'd just done, and he advised me that if I stuck to my present course, I could kiss goodbye to any lawsuit against Empire for wrongful termination.

I said that was fine with me, and asked him to send me a bill, which, knowing about Beth, he never did. Aside from his kindness, I had a lousy Christmas.

I came to be only four people away from the cashier in the line at the unemployment office. The lady in front of me shuffled forward. She was dragging a shopping bag along the floor. I glanced into the bag. It looked like a condensed version of somebody's attic.

There was a while there after I left Empire when I thought I might be in trouble. While Beth was sick, I'd started running in the early mornings to try to work off my anxiety. After she died, I stopped jogging and started drinking. After I left Empire, I really started hitting it, leaving unopened most of the packed boxes in the new apartment. Then one January night, driving home from a bar, I missed a kid on a bike by about half a Scotch.

When I got to the apartment, I threw up twelve or fifteen times and tried to drown myself in the shower. I climbed out and looked at myself in the mirror. I began taking stock. Thirty-plus, six feet two–plus. Unemployed and rapidly approaching unemployable. I'd spent most—hell, all—of my adult life in investigation work for Uncle Sugar or Empire. Six years earlier Empire had required all of us to obtain and maintain private-detective licenses from the Department of Public Safety. I knew three or four semireputable guys in the trade who could tell me how to get started and maybe even refer me a few clients. I decided it was time J. F. C. became his own man. With a little interim help from the unemployment-compensation folks.

The shopping-bag lady waddled past me. I reached the window, collected my $106.25, expressed my gratitude, and went home.

Second

THE bouncy voice on the other side of the fire alarm said, "Hi, John. This is Valerie Jacobs." The clock radio said eight-thirty; the sun in my bedroom window said A.M. Unfortunately, I had decided to cut back on my drinking slowly, and the Red Sox game on TV the night before had gone thirteen innings.

"Hi," I said quietly. "Who are you?"

"Fine, thanks," she replied, I guess because she thought I'd said "how" instead of "who." Maybe I had. "The school year's over, and I'm hoping this will be my best summer of all."

"That's nice," I said.

"Listen, John, I can tell I woke you up, and I'm sorry. I wanted to talk to you about a problem, but when I called Empire, they said you'd left the company. I'm not seeing Chuck anymore, so I didn't know."

Valerie. Valerie and Chuck. Sure. She was a teacher who'd been going out with one of the claims adjusters in the office. Beth and I had met her at a few company functions. In fact, I remembered she'd sent a condolence card just after Beth died.

"I'm a private detective now. In Boston."

"Oh, John, that's perfect! I know this is short notice, but so much time has gone by already. Could you meet me for lunch today? Around one?"

"Sure."

"How about L'Espalier?"

"Fine. You buyin'?"

"Put it on your expense account," she laughed, and hung up before I could tell her she definitely had overestimated my status in the profession.

I got up, vacillated over running, then finally laced my Brooks Villanovas. I pulled on a fading Tall Ships T-shirt from the Bicentennial summer and a pair of black gym shorts. I warmed up with loosening and stretching exercises for ten minutes and then went outside. It was a glorious June day, and the sidewalk was frying-pan hot. In Boston, we don't have spring; at some point in May, we jump from March to August.

I crossed over Storrow Drive on the pedestrian ramp and did a fairly leisurely two miles upriver and two miles back. As I recrossed the ramp toward Charles Street and the apartment, I watched the commuters inch by below me.

It had been only five months since I'd missed the kid on the bike, but I wasn't really struggling. In terms of conditioning (or reconditioning, if you insist), I'd been running three times a week, three to six miles each time. I'd been doing push-ups, sit-ups, and a little weight lifting. To try to regain some dangerousness, I began relearning jukado (a combination of judo, karate, and a number of other disciplines), which I'd picked up in the army. I even persuaded a police-chief friend of mine from Bonham (pronounced "Bonuhm," if you please), a town south and west of Boston, to let me use his department's pistol range.

In terms of business, the advent of no-fault divorce in Massachusetts had cut back considerably on that aspect of private investigating, which was fine by me. A friend in the trade had told me that the secret of survival was keeping the overhead down. He suggested I use a tape device on my telephone instead of an answering service, and he was proving to be right. I also operated out of my apartment, so I had no office expense.

A retired Boston cop who'd known my family was a security director for a suburban department store. He had thrown a few "inside-job" surveillances my way, and on one we'd actually nailed the dipping employee. I had been quietly blackballed in Boston insurance circles, which kept my unemployment compensation coming. However, one maverick investigator had brought me in as a consultant on a warehouse security problem, and I sewed it up nicely in enough days to pay the next three months' rent. In other words, although I wasn't exactly pressed for free time, I was getting by.

I stopped at the grocery store on the corner and bought a quart of orange juice, some doughnuts, a *Boston Globe* and a *New York Times*. I politely stayed downwind (actually down-air-conditioner) from the cashier. After I climbed the three flights to my apartment, I duplicated the pre-run exercises. I showered, shaved, downed my doughnuts, and dressed in my only gray slacks and blue blazer. I even wore a regimental tie. Peter Prep School goes to luncheon.

I sat in Public Garden for two hours, reading my

papers thoroughly in a way I'd never seemed able to while I was working. Funny, with my time my own and only food, shelter, and car insurance to worry about, I couldn't really look on my present occupation as working. By the time I finished the *Times*, it was 12:45, and I'd been panhandled three times. I walked down Arlington Street and toward the restaurant.

L'Espalier was then on the second floor of a building between Arlington and Berkeley streets on Boylston. It has since moved to Gloucester Street between Newbury and Commonwealth. It has also ceased serving lunch, to allow concentration on the magnificent dinner menu. The couple who own and manage the restaurant had lived above Beth and me in the condominium building. After Beth died, I'd wasted some beautiful afternoons over a carafe of house bordeaux while Donna and Moncef patiently looked on.

Donna greeted me at the entranceway and gave me a table for two in the corner. I'd just ordered a piña colada (without the kick) when Valerie walked in. I recognized her, but I realized I would have been hard put to describe her beforehand.

She stood about five-seven without the heels. She had long, curly-to-the-point-of-kinky auburn hair, a broad, open face, and a toothy smile. That may sound unkind; I don't mean it to be. Let's say she resembled Mary Tyler Moore in her late twenties. Her sundress hinted at small but nicely shaped breasts. The dress also hid most of her legs, which were slightly heavier than I would have recalled but appeared, thankfully, to be shaved. She was burdened with at least four store bags.

From the door, she gave me a wave that was a little too much "I'm-meeting-someone-in-a-nice-Boston-restaurant" and therefore not entirely for my benefit. She smiled at and said something to Donna and strode over toward me. I noticed that Donna was giving me a sardonic grin. I also noticed, as Valerie cleared the table before mine, that the bags she carried were from Lord & Taylor and Saks Fifth Avenue, labels out. I stood up.

"John, you've lost weight," she exclaimed.

"And teaching must be fairly profitable," I replied, nodding at her packages.

"Oh," she said with her smile, "this is my annual showboat excursion into the Big City. Usually I just barter my wares for dry goods at the general store."

She giggled, and so did I. Despite her first appearance, I remembered her as a pretty regular kid, and I decided she hadn't changed

She declined a cocktail. We ordered a bottle of white wine to be followed by a chicken luncheon for two. She said what she had to about Beth, and I did the same. The waiter brought and poured the wine. We talked about classrooms, the declining birth rate, and teacher lay-offs.

"So how goes the private-eye business?" she asked.

I exaggerated a little. I was relieved that she didn't ask for details.

"I'm sorry," I said finally, "but I don't recall exactly where it is that you're teaching."

A flicker of disappointment at the corners of her eyes? "Um," she said, "Meade, the Lincoln Drive Middle School. And that brings me to what I wanted to see you about. Do you know where Meade is?"

I did. "It's right next to Bonham, isn't it?"

She nodded as the waiter arrived with our chicken.

"If it's particularly gory, why don't we wait until after the meal?" I said.

"Oh, it's not," she replied quickly, and glanced down at the waiter's tray. "But let's not be rude to the chicken." I laughed and motioned to the waiter to begin serving.

The entrée was delightful, punctuated by few words. Valerie finished a bit before I did and fixed me with dark, dark brown eyes. "I can't really start at the beginning because I didn't know the family then," she said. "But this past year in class—I teach the eighth grade—I had a boy named Stephen Kinnington in my homeroom and English classes."

"Familiar name," I interjected as I finished the last of my chicken.

"I'm not surprised. His father, Judge Kinnington, was one of the youngest men ever to go on the bench, and his family has sort of, well, *ruled* Meade since long before I arrived. Anyway, Stephen's mother, Diane Kinnington, killed herself about four years ago by driving her Mercedes off a bridge and into the river. Apparently she boozed it up a lot, so no one knows whether it was accidental or intentional. It hit Stephen pretty hard, as you can imagine. I've talked with his fifth-grade teacher, Miss Pitts, who's retired now, and she said that his mother's 'activities,' as Miss Pitts put it, had appeared to be affecting Stephen for a long time prior to Mrs. Kinnington's actual death. I got the impression from Miss Pitts that by 'activities' something more than simple alcoholism was involved, if you know what I mean."

"I've read of such goings on in France," I said.

Valerie made a face and drove on. "Anyway, by the time I got Stephen this year, he seemed to be perfectly normal, though a little reserved around the other kids. By all tests, he was exceptionally bright. I mean a real brain trust. At the beginning of the year, he would ask me whether I'd read certain books. He had obviously read them, and they were way beyond eighth-grade level. He'd missed a year because of sickness, but he's still only fourteen. I sort of took it on myself to suggest to his father that perhaps Stephen should go to a private school with an accelerated program. But whenever I called his office at the courthouse, he wasn't available, and he never returned my calls."

"Don't you have some sort of parent-teacher conference during the year?"

"Yes, but he didn't appear for the first one I scheduled, and when I called his home that evening, he wasn't in. I was pretty upset, since those conferences are scheduled on my time, so I kind of demanded to speak with someone—the housekeeper answered the phone, you see—and that's how I came to meet Mrs. Kinnington."

"The judge remarried?" I asked.

"Oh, no, his mother—that is, the judge's mother and Stephen's grandmother, Eleanor Kinnington. Everyone calls her Mrs. Kinnington. She's a little tower of power, and she was ripping mad that the judge had skipped the appointment. She asked if it was convenient for me to come there for dinner the next evening to discuss Stephen. I said I'd be happy to come, but the judge wasn't there the next night, either, and Mrs. Kinnington apologized for him through clenched teeth.

"I had a terrific dinner and talk with her, though. She must be nearly eighty and needs hand braces, the kind polio victims use, to walk around. But she's really sharp. Anyway, she said the judge would never allow his son to go to a private school. I got the impression that it was for local political reasons, as if it would seem that the local public schools weren't good enough for a Kinnington. She encouraged me to help Stephen as much as I could. I got the feeling that she thought the wife's death was really a blessing in disguise.

"Anyway, after that I began giving Stephen some separate reading assignments that he really enjoyed. I also got to be good friends, in a formal sort of way, with Mrs. Kinnington, because we'd discuss Stephen from time to time."

Valerie paused for a moment to take a sip of wine. I found her way of running parenthetical thoughts and sentences together to be a little tough to follow, but oddly not tiresome.

"Um, I have to stop drinking this wine or I'll never stay straight enough to finish the story. Anyway, about two weeks ago, Stephen disappeared."

"Kidnapped?"

"Apparently not. It seems that he packed his things one afternoon and, well, left."

"You mean he ran away from home?"

"Well, yes, but not exactly. I mean, no neighbor saw him shuffling along the sidewalk with a stick and stuffed handkerchief over his shoulder. And he packed really thoroughly, as if he expected to go a long way for a long time.

"Has he been heard from?"

She shook her head as she stole another gulp of wine. "No, and the police haven't found a trace in two weeks."

"What police?"

"The local Meade police. Technically, I guess he's just a missing person, since there's no evidence of kidnapping. But there's been no publicity, so no one is on the lookout for him except some agency that the judge hired. You see—"

"Wait a minute. What agency?"

"Oh, somebody and Perkins on State Street."

"Sturney and Perkins, Inc. They're one of the best, Val."

She smiled. "But they haven't found anything. And I bet they're not nearly as good as you."

I set down my wine glass and fixed her with my best counselor's look. "Val, Sturney and Perkins have a substantial staff. In a specific crime-type case, sometimes one operative is better than an army. That's because he or she can get inside the investigation without causing ripples until he wants to make something happen. But a missing-person case requires a computer-type approach, assembling all the information you can from all sources and trying to blanket the areas he might be in with investigators, police and private."

"But then why haven't there been newspaper articles with pictures of him to help?" she asked, her eyes glittering.

"Maybe the police and Sturney, *et alia*, feel that publicity would just invite a lot of crank calls or start the wrong people looking for him."

"You mean like criminals the judge put away?" she asked.

"One example," I said.

"But right now he's out there with them anyway. I mean, he's in their element, where he's more likely to be hurt by someone who doesn't even know who he is."

She was becoming upset, so I decided to shift gears a little. "By the way, if his disappearance has been kept so much under wraps, how do you know about his packing and so forth?"

She blinked a few times and played with her nearly empty wine glass. "Well, that's how I came to see you.

Stephen didn't come to school for two days—you see, he took off just after final exams. Anyway, I called his house—I'd given up trying to reach his father—and Mrs. Kinnington told me all about it. We've talked almost every day since, and she was so upset last night, because nothing has happened, and I know I don't have the money to pay you, so . . . "

"So you sort of volunteered to be her cat's-paw and bring me into the case for her."

She looked at me with a smile somewhere between bleakness and mischief. "At least you think it's a case, huh?"

I put on a fake frown, and she laughed. "Oh, please, John, he's such a good, bright little kid. He's had such a tough time so far, with his mother and all, and I'm so afraid for him out there."

"Okay, okay," I said, and motioned to the waiter. "Let's have our salad, and then you call Mrs. Kinnington to set up an appointment."

She smiled and shook her hair and poured herself another glass of wine.

"Today's the judge's day for tennis, so he won't be home until at least seven. She's expecting you at four-fifteen."

Third

VALERIE wanted to drive me out to the Kinnington place, but I insisted that she merely lead me there and let me see Mrs. Kinnington alone. She reluctantly walked with me to a rent-a-car place in Copley Square (my ancient Renault Caravelle being in the shop awaiting a used A-frame from North Carolina). I rented a Mercury Monarch, and we bailed her car out of a parking garage.

We took the Mass Turnpike to Route 128, the elongated beltway around Boston. We were beating the high-tech rush hour by thirty minutes. After about six miles we took the exit after the one I used for Bonham and continued into Meade.

As we wound down the stylish country road, I began to get a better sense of the town. Meade was about as rural as its neighbor Bonham, but a good deal ritzier. In Bonham, there were big old farmhouses flanked by peeling, musty-looking barns with rusting agricultural machinery slumped in the yards. In Meade, there were big, skylighted farmhouses flanked by newly painted, too-red barns with burnished Mercedeses and Jags in the yards. I looked at myself in the rear-view mirror. Meade would happen to Bonham someday, and at that point I'd probably no longer be able to use the pistol range.

Val signaled a turn onto a private gravel road, then pulled past it to a stop. She stuck her head out the window and swiveled a hopeful face back toward me. I waved her on. She frowned and crunched some gravel on the shoulder as she accelerated out. I checked my watch. It was a shade after four, so I made the turn and weaved slowly upward through the trees.

As I approached it, the house appeared more modest than I had expected. It was a white colonial, with thin black shutters framing the smallish downstairs windows. No modern glass walls punched through here.

I swung around a wide circular drive with a small, nonspitting fountain in the center. I pulled past the fountain so that the Merc was headed out again. By the time I closed the car door, the main door to the house was open, and a middle-aged black woman stood frowning at me.

"Hello," I said, "I'm—"

"I don't want to know your name. I don't even know you're here. Mrs. Kinnington is upstairs. Follow me."

Maybe, I thought, it's my breath.

The central staircase was beautifully maintained, with a polished, curving mahogany handrail atop off-white pickets. The steps were mahogany under a narrow, oriental runner. I glanced left and right as we climbed the stairs. On one side I could see a living room with a large portrait of a young army officer over the mantel. On the other side was the corner of a dining room. Polished hardwood floors and no wall-to-wall, only old, tasteful orientals. A natural product of old, tasteful money.

At the top of the staircase was an invalid lift, a chair that would slide mechanically up and down on a floor-and-wall track. Through clever coloring, the wall tracks were almost invisible. We turned right, then left. There appeared to be a similar wing on the other side of the stairs. I realized that the house was a good deal bigger than it appeared from the driveway.

We entered a robin's-egg-blue bedroom that must have measured thirty by thirty feet. Sitting on a love seat, with a beautiful silver service on a low table in front of her, was a double for the late actress Gladys Cooper. A double except for the eyes, which were flinty-hard and so dark that there was no way to tell where the pupil stopped and the iris began. On one side of her rested a pair of metal braces; on the other was a Princess phone the color of the walls.

"Good afternoon, sir," she said. "Thank you, Mrs. Page; that will be all."

I half-turned, and Mrs. Page shot me a look that indicated that she was sorry her name had ever been mentioned in my presence. She closed the door behind her.

"No need to worry about Mrs. Page," she said in a tone she probably believed to be pleasant. "She and I have an understanding. Please sit down."

The least delicate-looking chair in the room had apparently been moved from a now-bare corner to a conversational distance from her. I took it.

"Will you have some tea?"

I declined.

She settled back with hers. "You look younger than I expected," she said from behind her teacup.

"It's the booze," I replied. "It acts as a preservative."

She sniffed a smile at me. "Middle-aged and impudent. Well, that's probably just the combination I require. Has Miss Jacobs fully informed you of what has happened?"

"Miss Jacobs has told me everything she believes is important."

A better smile this time, and the teacup was replaced on the tray. "Why don't we begin discussing what I feel is important, then?"

"Fine. Just so it doesn't interrupt our train of thought later, my fee is two hundred and fifty dollars per day, plus expenses."

"I trust then that you intend working on no other cases save this one?"

"By some frantic telephoning, I was able to clear my calendar."

"Continue."

"Second, the chances of one investigator finding

one boy two weeks after he has vanished, even assuming he hasn't been kidnapped, are very, very slim."

"He hasn't been kidnapped."

"What makes you so sure?"

"There has been no ransom note, and Stephen packed before he left."

"Both good reasons, Mrs. Kinnington, but I'm afraid the lack of a ransom note would be consistent with packing if someone were trying to give the impression that the boy had skipped on his own."

She broke eye contact and retrieved her teacup. "Could we please refer to my grandson as 'Stephen' rather than 'the boy'?" she said softly.

"Of course." A sincere emotion? Yes, all the more because while the voice changed, the face, more easily controlled, did not.

"I'm certain Stephen packed himself, because items are missing that another person, even his father, would never have thought to take."

I let the reference to the judge pass for the moment. "For instance?"

"Before we go any further, I really must give you some insight about Stephen. He is an exceptionally gifted child. He was reading at age three. I had feared so that his mother's behavior and the shock of her death would crush his talents. But if anything, his unfortunate home life seems to have spurred him. His teachers and I, recognizing his abilities, have given him more and more advanced materials to study and absorb. Given a few months of intensive study, I daresay he would be a better lawyer than—but I digress. The point I mean to make is that Stephen has the emotional and intellectual courage to strike out on his own. He would know exactly and concisely what he would need, and that is what he packed."

24

"What did he pack for?"

"Until my stroke, three years ago, I was an active camper. The judge despises the outdoors and would invent illness when he was younger to avoid coming with my husband and . . . and me.

"Stephen, however, seemed born with a love for the outdoors. He would walk the property here, approximately seventy-five acres, endlessly, as one season changed into another, observing the wildlife and plants. After my stroke, he would come in each day and describe to me what he'd seen and heard and touched. He became terribly interested in the wilderness, and with my help, he and I selected numerous books and items from L. L. Bean, Abercrombie, and other catalogs to prepare a wilderness-survival kit for him."

"And that's what he took with him?"

"Yes and no, Mr. Cuddy, and that's my point. What is missing is not his whole kit nor a random sampling of all the items he had. What he took were only the lightest components and the barest necessities. My memory is still perfectly sharp, and I'm sure only his hand or mine could have selected so carefully the items that are missing."

"Could you make a list of those, along with the clothes he was wearing and the clothes that are missing?"

She reached her hand down between the cushion and the couch and handed me a small envelope. "It's all in there."

"Do you have a picture of him?"

"The best one I have is in the envelope. I would appreciate your making copies and returning it to me as soon as possible."

"I'll do that." I opened the envelope and scanned

the list. It was written on rose-colored stationery with her name embossed on the top. The handwriting, now shaky, once must have won penmanship awards.

I studied the photograph. It showed a black-haired boy, whittling but looking up at the lens. The body was right, but the face was somber, joyless, and somehow not young.

"How long ago was this taken?"

"About six weeks. Stephen disappeared on Tuesday, June 12. The photograph was taken by his father, which explains Stephen's expression."

I slipped the photo back into the envelope. "Mrs. Kinnington, you don't speak as lovingly of your son as you do of Stephen. Was the judge the reason Stephen ran away?"

"I don't believe that is necessary for your task. Regardless of what Stephen's reasons were for leaving, I am convinced Stephen's father had nothing directly to do with Stephen's departure. Accordingly, I don't wish you to speak with the judge nor even allow him to become aware that you are pursuing the case on my behalf."

I cleared my throat. "Mrs. Kinnington, that's probably not possible. I'll have to ask some questions in this town about Stephen, and that fact is bound to get back to the judge. Aside from you and him, I can't think of anyone who would hire me to look for Stephen. He's bound to add it up."

Mrs. Kinnington fixed me firmly. "Nevertheless, I do not wish you to do anything that would specifically lead him to that conclusion."

"Mrs. Kinnington, I will do what I believe is best for finding Stephen. If that isn't acceptable to you, I'll walk right now. No charge."

She blinked and sighed. "Please do your best, then, to honor my wishes," she murmured.

"I will."

I mentally reviewed the topics I had wanted to cover with her. Two remained.

"I have only a few more questions for now, Mrs. Kinnington. One is about Stephen's institutionalization after his mother died."

Her eyes sharpened again with her voice. "That was years ago. What could it possibly have to do with his disappearance now?"

"Frankly, I don't kow. But it seems to me something must have happened to cause Stephen to take off. Perhaps that something isn't a new occurrence but rather a recurrence from those days."

She sighed again. The institutionalization appeared to be as difficult for her to discuss as it must have been for Stephen to experience. "I had very little to do with that. I was out of the country when Stephen's mother died, and the judge's actions were *fait accompli* by the time I got back." She adopted the hard tone again. "I distrust psychiatrists and other so-called mental health professionals. I believe that love, not analysis, is what Stephen needed. In any case, however, the name of the sanatorium was Willow Wood. It was in the Berkshires near Tanglewood. I don't recall the town, but I doubt it would do you any good to find it. I'm sure the judge would have sealed things up tightly to avoid any adverse publicity."

I thought it over. She was probably right about the sanatorium itself. Then I recalled something a doctor once told me when I was visiting Beth in the hospital.

"Mrs. Kinnington, it seems that I've heard a psychiatric hospital usually does follow-up treatment on a released patient. Since the sanatorium must be a hundred miles from here, do you recall any local psychiatrist seeing Stephen after he was sent home?"

She regarded her teacup for a moment. "Yes, yes, I do. He was in Brookline. Stern? No, no, Stein. That was the name. Dr. David Stein."

I nodded. "Could you call him and authorize him to speak with me about Stephen?"

"Mr. Cuddy, I want one point to be absolutely clear," she said, again hardening her voice. "I will not have those days reopened. The judge and I would agree on that, though he for selfish reasons of publicity and I for concern about Stephen. Is that understood?"

"Mrs. Kinnington, if your concern for Stephen is so strong, I would think you'd want me to reopen anything I had to in order to bring him home safely."

She locked eyes for another moment, then relented once more. "This is all so . . . difficult to deal with. We had all thought him to be . . . Very well. I see your point. I will call this Dr. Stein."

"By 'this Dr. Stein,' do I take it you never met him?"

"That's correct. I've a vague recollection of speaking to him once on the telephone."

"In that case," I said, "could you give me a brief letter of introduction, preferably on some of your stationery?"

"Certainly," she swiveled and scooped up her walking braces in her right hand.

I extended my right hand. "Do you need some help?" I asked.

She shook her head as she maneuvered the braces to the sides of her chair. "Never ask someone in a wheelchair, which I was, or on braces if they 'need some help.' Psychologically, they can't answer yes to that question."

"Well, then, can I give you a hand?"

She rewarded me with her faint smile. "Better. But

no, thank you," she said as she levered herself up to a standing position. "I prefer to have tea at a tea table and to write letters at a desk. This way, please."

Her legs moved stiffly in lockstep with the thrust of her shoulders and braces. She stopped at a Governor Winthrop desk, which looked to my untutored eye to be made of curly maple and therefore probably even more antique than the rest of the place. She lowered the drawbridge writing surface, revealing a desk fountain pen. She eased into the chair, leaning her braces against the wall, out of the way but within reach.

"Now," she said, tugging open a shallow drawer and removing another sheet of the rose-colored stationery, "what shall I write?"

I slowly dictated a form of authorization and release, which I had seen often enough at Empire to know by heart. It authorized Dr. Stein to reveal Stephen's confidences and to allow me to review medical and hospital records, releasing him from liability if he did so. She signed it and handed it to me.

"Is there anything else?" she said.

"If you would call Dr. Stein and let him know I'm coming?"

"Certainly."

I put the letter and the envelope in my breast pocket. "One last thing. Given your knowledge of what Stephen knows about the wilderness, do you have any ideas about where he might go?"

She looked up and smiled wanly. "We maintained a veritable atlas of topographical maps of the Eastern seaboard in his room, to plan or just fantasize about future trips. They are all still there, which probably means he found a way to copy one before he left. He could be anywhere."

I nodded. "I can reach you by telephone here?"

"During the day," she said. "If you need me at night, please call Miss Jacobs and have her call me. I will then call you when everyone else is asleep."

I nodded again. "I'd like to speak to Mrs. Page now."

"That's not necessary, Mr. Cuddy. Stephen disappeared on her day off. I've already questioned her thoroughly, and she knows nothing."

And, I gathered, if she did know anything, Mrs. Page wouldn't tell *me*.

I said goodbye and went out into the hall. I retraced my steps down the stairs, and as I reached the front door I was aware of Mrs. Page behind me. At least she hadn't frisked me to check for the family silver.

I smiled at her, and she shook her head. As I went through the door, she began closing it behind me. "Blakey's gonna eat you alive," she said in a tsk-tsk whisper.

I considered knocking on the door, but I didn't think she'd elaborate even if she opened it again. I got in the Merc, drove down to the main road, and swung back toward Boston and opposite the first strains of the westward commuter traffic. Almost immediately, a black sedan swerved into my lane and I had to cut onto the shoulder. I glared over at the driver. My eyes caught about one frame of a beefy, stupid face before he was past me. I wrestled my car back onto the roadbed.

I got to Route 128, but instead of turning north toward Mass Pike and the fast way into Boston, I turned south and picked up the usually mis-named expressway, which leads into the city from the southeast. This looked as if it was going to be an effort-intensive case, and I wanted to pay a visit first.

Fourth

"Just carnations." I set them down and stepped back. "Mrs. Feeney said the roses at the flower market were tired-looking." I felt too distant standing up, so I squatted down on my haunches.

"Remember Valerie Jacobs, Chuck Craft's friend? Well, she's brought me a case, and it's a beaut! Rich family and all kinds of troubles. The grandmother, you'd like. Good Yankee, you'd call her. The grandson I haven't met yet, and won't, if I don't roll pretty hard and fast on finding him. Still, he sounds like the type you'd have liked too. Serious, studied, and quiet. Just like me." We laughed.

I stared at the carnations for a while. I began blinking rapidly. We talked inside for a bit.

"So. I'm afraid I won't be back for a while. I'll see you when the case is over. Or sooner, if I hit a problem. Just like always."

I straightened up and turned around to walk back down the path. A teenager holding a rake and wearing a maintenance shirt and dungaree cut-offs gave me a funny look. I didn't recognize him. Summer help, probably, and young. Too young to know anything. Especially anything about cemeteries.

When I got back to Charles Street I put the Merc up at the garage on the riverside and grabbed a steak at the charcoal place that was then near the intersection of Beacon. In the apartment I made a screwdriver (the orange juice makes me feel healthy) and played back my telephone tape. The only caller was Valerie. She wanted me to call her back and tell her about my interview with Mrs. Kinnington. Instead, I dialed Chief Maslyk's home number in Bonham and asked him if he'd like to fire a few strings with me at the range tomorrow. He said he couldn't but would be available the next day, around 9:30. He'd meet me there.

After I hung up, I thought about Valerie. I downed the second half of my screwdriver and left the telephone on tape rather than on ring for the rest of the night.

Fifth

I got up at 6:30 on Thursday morning and did what I call my double-declining calisthenics. I start with fifty push-ups, one hundred arm rotations, and one hundred fast-flapping over-and-under motions. For the last, I stand, swing my arms horizontally forward with fists clenched until they pass each other. Then I swing them back hard, trying to touch them behind my back. Then I swing them forward again, and so forth. After I finish, I repeat the series, halving the number of repetitions of each exercise. I then did a fast (for me) three miles along the river and wolfed down the "farmhand breakfast" (three eggs, four sausages, hash browns, toast, juice, coffee, parsley, oregano, and God knows what else) at a luncheonette on Cambridge Street.

I got back to the apartment and cleaned up. I checked the phone tape. Valerie had called again and said that the reason I couldn't reach her last night was because she and a girlfriend had gone to a drive-in and she was leaving for the beach and wouldn't be in until six and would I please call her then and she . . . at which point, mercifully, the tape's maximum run was reached. Feeling vaguely relieved, I reset the tape, dressed in a conservative dark suit as the concerned father of an accused delinquent might, and set off for Meade District Court.

As I turned into the court parking lot, I noticed it was almost three-quarters full at 8:30 A.M. I wanted to at least get a look at His Honor before I started after his son. Also, because of my understanding with Mrs. Kinnington, I thought I ought to do my observing before I did any poking around that would identify me for him.

The courthouse looked spanking new. It was red brick and from the exterior had some stylish peaks that implied cathedral ceilings inside. As I walked from the lot toward the door, I caught a glimpse of a court officer with a hand-held metal detector at the entrance, thoroughly going over an obvious lawyer type carrying an attaché case.

I immediately spotted a terrible scuff on my right shoe, whipped out a handkerchief, and failed miserably to remove it. Nervously shaking my head, I walked quickly back to my car, where I opened the trunk, reached in for an imaginary rag, and slipped my wood-handled .38 Smith & Wesson Chief's Special and clip-on holster from over my right hip. I fussed with my shoe and then tucked the pistol and holster completely under the plastic rug in the trunk before closing the lid and retracing my steps toward the courthouse door. Ever since the bombing at the superior court in Boston several years before, varying degrees of security had been imposed on entry to the commonwealth's courthouses, but virtually none included checking out well-dressed, distinguished-looking, mature men. Apparently Judge Kinnington's building, which he ran as presiding judge, was the exception.

I passed inspection and milled around with the crowd inside the lobby of the courthouse. As I bumped my way up and down the broad corridor, I realized there were two courtrooms on the main floor and at least one other (based on signs at the staircases) on the second floor. I drifted into the clerk's office and casually asked who was sitting in the First Session (Massachusetts legalese for courtroom number one, which is usually the courtroom to which all cases report and from which all cases are assigned to other courtrooms for hearing). A faded disco queen behind the desk said "Judge Kinnington, of course," and I thanked her and went back into the mob just as a short, elderly court officer began shrieking.

"First Session, First Session, court is coming in. All criminal business. Court is coming in." The doors of the First Session swung open, and an architectural vacuum cleaner sucked virtually all the inhabitants of the corridor inside. The only exceptions were a few lawyers who looked well-to-do and vaguely uncomfortable, which probably meant they were out here defending General Motors or Boston Edison on some minor but time-consuming civil matter.

I became part of the wedge cutting its way into the First Session. The courtroom was like a church, with one of the cathedral ceilings I'd spotted from the outside. The doors opened onto a wide center aisle, and the seating for the public was on high-backed benches, rather like Catholic pews without the kneelers. The center aisle ended at a gateway in a fence. The fence is the bar enclosure, so-called by lawyers because usually only members of the bar may sit within it. The fencing reminded me very much of a half-scale model of the balustrade on the stairway in the judge's house. Past the bar enclosure, which was sunken like a split-level living room, was the bench, raised like a pulpit.

I spotted two especially scuzzy-looking early-teenaged boys sitting near the aisle. I sat down next to them. I practiced a concerned glance in their direction. They returned a disgusted look, probably thinking that I was there on a morals charge.

"Courrrrrrrt!" bellowed the little court officer, and the congregation rose as the Honorable Willard J. Kinnington fairly scooted from a door to the right side of the bench and ascended. Possibly he moved so quickly because he was only barely medium height and didn't wish to advertise it. He had slightly graying, blondish-red hair and was wearing amber horn-rimmed glasses. He clutched a small loose-leaf book in his right hand; with his black robes this gave him the appearance of a new parish priest slightly late for his first mass. Once on the bench, however, he fixed the entire courtroom with a baleful eye. With the added height of the raised bench, he now looked as though he could jump center for the Celtics. He bowed his head as the court officer intoned the full salutation. The courtroom clock showed 9:00 A.M. on the nose.

"Hear ye, hear ye, hear ye. All those having business before this, the Fourth District Court of Western Norfolk, now sitting in Meade, within in and for our county of Norfolk, the Honorable Willard J. Kinnington presiding, draw near, give your attention, and you shall be heard. God save the commonwealth of Massachusetts and this honorable court. Be seated."

I watched the judge as the court officer spoke; he didn't twitch during the entire soliloquy. In Massachusetts, there is a district-court system, which handles lesser matters, and a superior court system, which handles graver matters. Each district court is in an important town and includes several smaller towns within its jurisdiction. The superior courts are countywide courts. Until court reorganization becomes a functioning reality, the major difference between the two systems is that whereas the district court is apparently less prestigious, the superior-court judges have to ride the circuit, rotating every month or so all over the state. The district-court judges sit almost exclusively in one district court. Accordingly, some district-court judges, appointed for life, have built up substantial little fiefdoms over which they exercise almost unbridled control. I'd been in a dozen district courts and every superior court in eastern Massachusetts during my time with Empire. Although the full "Hear ye, hear ye" salutation is occasionally heard in superior court, I'd never before heard it used in a district court.

When the court officer ended, the judge sat down briskly and spoke a name quickly. The clerk had materialized in the wooden kangaroo's pouch immediately in front of the judge. He turned to Kinnington and began giving short, nervous answers to whatever questions the judge was asking.

Meanwhile, I caught sight of the back of a huge court officer who was sliding down the left-hand side aisle toward the judge's bench. He looked to be my height, but he was enormously thick across the back and bottom. He clicked open a side gate and entered the bar enclosure and moved up next to the clerk, who literally cringed away from him. Seeing him standing with his back to me and looming over the clerk, I pushed him up to six feet five. The giant's head bobbed up and down a little, as though he were talking. The judge's expression clouded, then cleared, and he muttered something to the giant. The giant nodded and backed away as the clerk called the first case.

A couple in front of me popped up with their son and blocked my view of the bench momentarily. They said their lawyer would be late, the judge asked the clerk if the lawyer had called the clerk's office, and the clerk said no. At that point the judge stated that their son's case would not be heard until 3:00 P.M. The father began to say something, but the clerk had already begun calling the next case.

As the trio hesitatingly sat back down, I saw the giant court officer in the side aisle pull even with my row and roll his gaze toward me as he walked back toward the only public entrance. His was the beefy, now not-quite-as-stupid face I'd seen in the car that had swerved at me the day before. He had a fringe of wispy blond hair around, and combed in ridiculously long strands across, his balding head. I didn't follow him with my eyes to the back of the room, but no sound came from the central door, which had squeaked a bit when opened by a latecomer a moment before. So much for my concerned-parent cover.

The next case was a Bonham police matter. The defendant's name was called, and the defendant and her attorney answered "Ready." No one, however, answered for the Bonham police, which, like most Massachusetts departments, prosecutes its own minor cases through a senior officer instead of tying up an assistant district attorney. A young, clean-cut guy within the bar enclosure (who turned out to be the Meade police prosecutor) stood up haltingly. He said, "Your Honor, I believe the Bonham police prosecutor is on the telephone arranging to bring in a witness." The judge glared down at him. "Case dismissed for lack of prosecution." I was stunned, but the young cop/prosecutor gamely tried a stall. "If Your Honor please. I can run back and—"

"Case dismissed!" boomed the judge, whose microphone was set, I suspect, a bit higher than anyone else's. The defendant and her lawyer got the hell out as fast as their feet would carry them.

And so it went. Of the twenty or so preliminary rulings I saw Kinnington make, at least six were similarly outrageous; yet he seemed to favor neither police nor defendants as a class. Each decision seemed exactly arbitrary, depending upon which party happened to appear to be giving the most affront to the judge's sense of how his time was to be used. I'm sure all six rulings were technically defensible. The point was that it was clear to everyone in the courtroom that the rulings were unfair and showed an incredible disregard for common sense.

I almost forgot. About six names (or three minutes) after the "case-dismissed" defendant, the central doors squeaked and a fiftyish, crew-cut guy in a brown double-knit blazer and baggy blue slacks hustled down the center aisle. I recognized him from the Bonham pistol range. He entered the bar enclosure and sat down hurriedly next to the young police prosecutor who'd stood up for him. The young one whispered to him. The old one turned to him with a look of disbelief on his face and half-rose from his chair. He sunk back down, faced front, and bowed his head. He then pounded the counsel table three times silently with his fist.

After the criminal cases had been called, the judge muttered something to the clerk, who turned to the judge and then turned back around with a surprised look on his face. "Court will recess for thirty minutes," he announced.

"All rise," shouted the elderly court officer as the judge scampered off the bench as quickly as he had ascended it and exited through the same door.

"Shit, man, we're gonna be here all fuckin' day," said the kid next to me to his friend as they got up and edged past me. About half the courtroom's population decided to do the same. I could feel the exodus clearing from the aisle, when a five-pound ham dropped on my shoulder. A gruff, egg-breathed voice said, "His Honor wants to see you in his chambers. Now."

I put on my most indifferent face and swiveled my head around. The giant's eyes were small and mean.

"I don't expect any special treatment, you know," I said mildly.

"Now."

I got up, and we walked abreast to a side door just forward of the right-hand seating area. I decided Giant was pushing six feet seven and maybe three hundred pounds. Giant used a key on the door. I moved before he could shove me through it. We entered a narrow corridor with PRIVATE stenciled on the painted walls. We made a sharp left and walked into a small outer office with a striking brunette secretary behind the reception desk. She gave me a quick look, as if she didn't want to be able to say later on that she recognized the body. Giant rapped a knuckle twice on the heavy-looking inner door and then pushed it open and motioned me in ahead of him. I walked in and glimpsed reddish hair behind the cloud of light blue cigar smoke hanging over a big desk. Then I was whirled around against the wall. I heard the door slam, and Giant said, "Assume the position."

I did so, with my hands outstretched on the wall, and Giant spread my legs a little wider. He locked one foot inside my right one and gave me a rough upper-body patdown.

When I was in army officer training, a military-police major always said to be sure to check a man's crotch for a weapon. When I was actually in the field, a military-police sergeant showed me how to bring the frisking hand up just right tô ring the friskee's chimes without any abrupt motion being apparent to an onlooker. I looked down as Giant started his hand up the inside of my right calf, saw the telltale turning of his wrist, and shifted my weight to the left just in time to catch most of his goose on my inner right thigh. Nevertheless, I heard a gentle tinkle of bells.

Giant snickered and moved back from me as I straightened up.

"He's clean, Your Honor," he said—"and smart."

"Please be seated, Mr. Cuddy."

No surprise there. Giant had probably read my plates when I pulled out of the judge's driveway yesterday. One call to the Registry of Motor Vehicles, one call to the Boston police, and one call by them to the Copley Square rent-a-car would have produced the information. Still, I had a feeling that Mrs. Kinnington would be disappointed in me. I also didn't like being roughhoused, even a little, by Giant. But I liked the judge's style sufficiently less that I maintained my composure and dignity. Which is a roundabout way of saying that I sat.

"Why were you visiting my mother yesterday?"

"Does Baby Huey have to hear all this?" I asked. I heard Giant suck in his breath behind me, as though he'd been waiting thirty years for somebody to call him that.

"Officer Blakey will stay." Well, one question answered. I must have missed the nameplate on the blue pup tent with sleeves that Blakey wore.

The judge continued, "By the way, I am sorry about the search, but no security system, even ours, is foolproof. I'm sure you understand." He smiled and gestured to a box on his desk. "Would you care for a cigar?"

"No."

The smile evaporated and was replaced by the case-dismissed look. "Why were you visiting my mother?"

"If you must know, we had a date for racquetball."

The judge's eyes glanced up and then down. The ham applied itself to my shoulder again and, this time, started to squeeze. The initial pain was welcomely replaced by a spreading numbness.

"By the way," I said through reasonably unclenched teeth, "did you hear the one about the Long Island judge who couldn't stand lousy coffee?" I was referring to a judge in New York who some years earlier had had his bailiffs handcuff a guy selling coffee outside his courthouse and drag him in to explain why the coffee was, in the opinion of the judge, so rotten. I couldn't remember what had happened to that judge, but apparently Kinnington did, because he waved Blakey off. My happy blood sang on its way back to my shoulder.

"Mr. Cuddy, I do not wish to see you around my property or my family again. Ever. Do I make myself clear?"

"I've understood every word you've said, Judge," I said as I stood and, not having been knocked down, turned and walked to the door. Blakey backed up, keeping two paces away from me, and opened the door for me.

"See ya around the quad, Cuddly Bear," I said softly to Blakey as I exited past him.

"Remember," said Blakey, just as softly.

In the court lobby I stopped at an enclosed pay phone. I called information, got the number I wanted, and dialed it.

"Sturney and Perkins, good morning."

"Good morning. This is John Francis calling from Judge Kinnington's court." I never like to tell a lie. "The judge and I were just speaking about a confidential matter that one of your people is handling, but frankly, the investigator's name has slipped my mind."

"Just a moment, please." There was a click, then dead space, then another click.

"That would be Ms. DeMarco, but I'm afraid she won't be in until two. Can I give her a message?"

"Gee," I said in my best Andy Hardy voice, "that's inconvenient for telephoning. The judge is in the next room. Hold on." I drummed my fingers through one verse of Eleanor Rigby so the no-doubt harried receptionist, when I got her back on, would not want to talk very long. I resumed. "Okay, I can be there at two-thirty. Just leave a message that I'll see her then."

"Fine. Thank you," said the receptionist crisply, and hung up.

I left the courthouse, retrieved my .38 from the

trunk, and got into the Mercury. It was only 10:10. The cat being out of the bag, I decided to rattle some more local cages before driving in to see Ms. De-Marco. I crisscrossed the downtown area of Meade until I spotted the police station. I parked (no meters) and went inside.

Sixth

THE desk sergeant blinked twice at me. "What did you say, buddy?" he asked.

I decided against raising my voice. "I said, could I please see whoever's in charge of Judge Kinnington's son's case."

"Sit down over there." I sat down on a bench seat across the small anteroom. The desk sergeant made an internal call while I gave him one of my best Gaelic smiles.

The desk sergeant clamped his hand over the mouthpiece of the phone. I hoped he wasn't going to yell anything confidential to me, since you have to cover both ends of the receiver to be sure the other party on the line can't hear what you're saying. "What's your name?"

"John Francis Cuddy, Sergeant."

He repeated the words into the phone. The sergeant said, "Right" and hung up. "The Chief will be back to me in a few minutes."

"Thank you, Sergeant," I said, and waited. Sergeants in every hierarchy love it when you call them by their title.

Five minutes later, the sergeant's phone rang. He picked it up and said, "Yes, Chief." Just then a young, short, and squat uniformed officer came through the front door. The sergeant hung up.

"Hey, Dexter, show Mr. Cuddy here to the chief's office."

The short, squat one stopped, nearly came to attention, and motioned to me. "Follow me, sir."

"Thank you, Sergeant," I repeated as I moved into the corridor.

"This is it, sir," said my guide as he gestured to a newly painted door.

"Thank you, Dexter."

"Yes, sir," he beamed, pushing out his chest. I was certain that he was somebody's nephew.

I knocked and heard a near-human growl from behind the door. I entered the office.

There was a nameplate on the desk that said SMOL-LETT. No rank or title, just Smollett. The plate was old and worn-looking. I got the impression the chief had bought it when he first came on the force, because he was old and worn-looking too. He had a voice that sounded like a '47 Nash without the mufflers.

"What do you want?" he said. I decided to sit down anyway.

"I want to speak with whoever's looking into Stephen Kinnington's disappearance."

"It's a missing-person case," he said, folding his hands, gnarled by arthritis, in front of him on the desk. "It's been looked into."

"Then can I look at the reports and talk to the investigating officer?"

"Why?" he asked, quite reasonably.

"Because I've been retained to find him," I replied.

"I wanna know who retained you."

"Why?" I asked, quite reasonably.

"Get out," he said, his eyes bulging a bit.

"Look, Chief," I said with some heat, "I've talked with the boy's grandmother, father, and now the chief of police of the town he skipped from. And so far all I'm getting told is to butt out. Now, if this were a criminal case, I could see it. The too-many-cooks theory. But with a missing person, the more knowledgeable people looking, the more likely it is somebody'll find something."

"Get out," he said again, his folded hands trembling a little.

I complied.

Seventh

AFTER I left the police station, I drove around Meade for an hour, just taking streets to see where they went and to get an idea of how many ways there might be for a fourteen-year-old boy to leave town. Even Meade's finest must have checked with bus drivers and the few cabs that plied the town. My guess was a cross-country hike until he was out of Meade and then maybe hitchhiking northwest to Worcester, northeast to Boston, or even southeast to Providence, Rhode

Island. From any city, his transportation opportunities were limitless. Even with publicity, the chances that someone would come forward to say, "Yeah, I picked up the kid," were astronomically small. Without publicity, there was no chance at all to trace his route. I was going to have to be very lucky and hope that I could deduce what city he'd chosen as his jumping-off point.

I cut short my wanderings and drove to the outskirts of Brookline, a beautiful bedroom suburb of Boston, but really a small city in its own right. I stopped at a telephone booth in a gas station.

The telephone book showed two Dr. D. Steins in Brookline but one was eliminated by his D.D.S. degree. Dr. Stein the psychiatrist was in a large, old stone medical building on Beacon Street across from the 1200 Beacon Motel. I eased the rent-a-car into one of the slanted center divider parking spaces, crossed the street, and entered the foyer.

I found Stein's door on the fourth floor and opened it. The foyer below and the hallway above were nondescript, but the psychiatrist's waiting room was elaborately furnished with a comfortable-looking sofa and four easy chairs arranged around a midsize oriental rug. The walls were a soft beige, with nonstrident landscapes and seascapes. If Dr. Stein intended his patients' surroundings to be soothing, his intention was successfully realized.

As I closed the door, I heard a low-toned bong. There was no receptionist, and indeed no desk or interior window for a receptionist. I was halfway to the inner office door when it opened.

"Yes?" said a tallish, slim man about forty. His initial smile of greeting faded as he failed to place me. He had a beard that was redder than the moplike sand-colored hair on his head.

"Dr. Stein?" I said.

"Yes."

"I'm John Cuddy. I believe Mrs. Kinnington called you?"

"Kinnington? She may have. I've been in group most of the morning. Kinnington?"

"I have a letter from her." I lifted it from my jacket pocket and handed it to him. He looked down at it.

"Yes, well . . ." He seemed only to skim the letter, but he nevertheless kept it in his hand when he looked back up. "I'll have to check my service. I never take calls when I'm in group. I'll be another fifteen minutes or so and then I can see you. Please sit down and I'll be back to you."

He withdrew into the inner office and closed the door. I sat down and scanned his eclectic magazine collection. I flipped through two old *New Yorker* magazines (which I read only for the cartoons) and was halfway through my third *Field and Stream* article (in their largemouth bass annual issue) when the inner door reopened and a string of two men and three women of varying ages filed out. From the distrustful looks they gave me as they passed, I think the waiting room's soothing qualities were pretty well wasted on them.

Stein was last out. He smiled at me and beckoned. I followed him in. Seating himself in a highback chair behind his desk, he bade me sit as well, so I dragged a visitor's lowback up to the front of the desk.

"I am sorry about disturbing you before," I said.

He waved me off as he sank, somewhat relieved, into his desk chair. "Not at all, not at all. In fact, despite what they say in clinic, I think an *occasional* interruption may be good for a group." He shot me a mischievous smile. "It's certainly good for me."

I smiled back. He reached for the telephone and hit

one button. "Checking my service," he said to me as an aside.

He spoke with the service for a while, taking down several quick notes on a pad. He said, "She did?" several times, then said thank you and hung up.

"Well," he said to me, "it seems your Mrs. Kinnington was quite insistent on reaching me. Virtually threatened my service with legal action if she were not put through."

"She's a very determined woman. And quite concerned about Stephen."

"Stephen, Stephen, yes, yes," he said as he looked at Mrs. Kinnington's letter again, and then rose and crossed to one of six file cabinets in the room. He pulled back a drawer, retrieved a file, and, opening it, returned to his seat.

As he turned the pages of the file, he spoke to me. "Mrs. Kinnington says in her note only that Stephen is missing. According to the file here and my recollection as well, Stephen's father was the family member most involved with Stephen's . . . ah, stay at Willow Wood."

I chose my words carefully. "Mrs. Kinnington was out of the country at the time. Both she and the judge are doing everything possible to locate him. You are just one link, but perhaps an important one, in that chain."

"Yes, yes, of course." Whatever momentary reticence he had had now seemed to dissolve. "Well then, how can I help you?"

I breathed an inner sigh of relief and plunged on. "We don't know why Stephen has disappeared. We thought you might be able to give us some idea."

Stein pursed his lips and flipped back to the front of the file. "According to my records, I last saw Stephen over three years ago. Aside from my file entries, I really have little recollection of him."

I leaned forward a bit. "What I am really interested in is why Stephen, after apparently doing so well for so long, suddenly does an about-face. Now, it may have been a new occurrence and it may have been a recurrence of something from his past. If we know what caused him to act, we may have a starting point for tracing him."

Stein tented his fingers and gave me a superior smile. "That's assuming that he departed of his own accord. Has that been established?"

"Not conclusively, but all the available evidence points toward his having run away rather than to kidnapping."

Stein nodded. He looked to his left and again re-read Mrs. Kinnington's letter. He seemed to be trying to memorize it. "I assume that time is of the essence, as the lawyers say?"

"Yes. The longer it takes us to find the key, the lower our chances of finding the boy."

Stein came to his decision and swung his desk chair and the folder around sideways. "Let's go through the file." I hitched my chair around so that we sat side by side at the narrow end of the desk.

The file was in reverse chronological order, so that you had to read from the bottom of the lower page to the top of the higher page. That awkwardness mastered, it took relatively little time to review.

Stephen was signed into Willow Wood by his father within twenty-four hours of his mother's death. He was diagnosed catatonic upon his arrival, and was treated with half a dozen drugs over the first two months. He slowly came out of the trance, showing exceptional manual dexterity and imagination.

Group therapy efforts were aborted nearly as soon as they were begun, Stephen preferring individual sessions, though not really coming around to any one analyst or therapist. The entries suggested Stephen most enjoyed outdoor activities and the library, shunning team sports and leadership roles.

"What kind of place is Willow Wood?" I asked.

Stein shrugged. "It's a low-security, very prestigious facility. In the old parlance, it would have been a sanatorium. It is set on the grounds of a beautiful estate about eight miles from Tanglewood. A friend of mine from medical school is head of staff there. Quite a plum position, but she was a superior doctor at a time when few women were entertained in medical school. She refers me all her discharging patients who are returning to the Boston area."

"There doesn't appear to be any indication of who referred the judge to Willow Wood."

"No, but any knowledgeable psychiatrist would know of Sarah—that's my classmate. Sarah might have a recollection of it, but surely it would be easier for you to just ask the judge."

"Right," I said, hopefully not too quickly. "Tell me about the course of care at Willow Wood, generally."

"Well, the course of care varies, of course, with the condition being treated. Willow Wood specializes, so to speak, in difficult, long-term cases of seriously ill, but not, dangerous individuals."

"Arts, crafts, and canoeing versus straitjackets and shock treatment?"

Stein snorted. "In a blunt sort of way, yes."

I returned to the file. Stephen seemed to improve month by month, if you compared a given week's entry to one four or five weeks later. The drugs dropped off, and the assessments of his progress steadily rose. About eight months after his initial admission, he was released to his father, with a forwarding referral to Dr. Stein.

I looked up at him. "Doctor, I don't quite understand something from the records here. What exactly was wrong with Stephen?"

"Well," said Stein, clearing his throat and shuffling through the file, "it's often difficult to diagnose exactly what was 'wrong' with a patient. One treats the apparent condition, or symptom, if you like, and then varies the treatment if earlier efforts prove unsuccessful. As you can see, Stephen was catatonic upon arrival at Willow Wood. Then slowly, by an evolving alternation of drugs, counseling, and therapeutic activities, he came back to us, so to speak."

"In layman's terms, you varied your prescriptions until he seemed to come out of it."

"Yes, but that can pretty generally be said about any patient."

"Then you can't really be sure of what was wrong with him to start with."

"Well, not in some microscopically, conclusively proved sense, no. When Stephen arrived at Willow Wood, he was literally in a trance. One can only identify the symptom or condition. One can't, despite magazine and television to the contrary, ever be sure of what's 'wrong with him,' in the sense I think you mean it."

I let it lay there while I returned to the file. The remaining pages were pale blue. "Are these blue pages yours?"

"Yes," he said, hopscotching with a pointed finger. "I first saw Stephen there, then a week later, then two weeks later, then one month later."

I read his entries. To me they seemed the sort of bland evaluation an assistant principal might give a kindergarten teacher. Stein's notes indicated good re-adjustment to home life, eagerness to return to school, intellectual curiosity, etc.

"I take it you came to no independent diagnosis of Stephen's illness."

"Well, no, but perhaps for a different reason. You see, by the time he came to me, he was no longer exhibiting any symptoms of any condition. He appeared to be a normal, well-adjusted boy of"—he consulted his entries—"ten, nearly eleven years old. Since he wasn't sick, so to speak, there was nothing to diagnose. Hence only the few, increasingly spaced visits."

"Do I understand then, Doctor, since neither Willow Wood nor you determined what was wrong with him, you don't know for sure that his mother's going off the bridge caused it?"

Stein blinked several times, and his mouth opened before he began to speak. Then he lapsed into a smile and gave me a patronizing look. "Given the chronological proximity of the event and the onset of the condition, what else could have caused it?"

I thanked him for his time and left.

Eighth

I drove into downtown Boston and parked on the fourth floor of the Government Center Garage. I walked through the new Faneuil Hall Market area. Although the renovated space opened in 1976, I grew up in old Boston, so I'll probably always call it the new market.

I stopped at my camera shop, where Danny promised me he'd have fifty copies of Stephen's photo for me within an hour. I moved down State Street.

Sturney and Perkins, Inc., was in an old, tasteful building near the waterfront. I took the elevator to the tenth floor. Sturney and Perkins occupied about half of it, the kind of offices a good, medium-sized Boston law firm would have had twenty years ago, before the glass-eyed skyscrapers opened.

"John Francis to see Ms. DeMarco."

The receptionist gave me an uncertain look and dialed two digits. Her telephone had a cover on the mouthpiece, which prevented me from hearing what she said into it. She hung up.

"I'll take you down myself." As we wound down a labyrinthine corridor, I thought it odd that she would leave her post. She showed me into a spacious, leather-done corner office with a harbor view. A tall, graying man who looked like an ex-navy commander stood from behind an expensive desk.

"Mr. Cuddy, this is Nancy DeMarco. I'm Charles Perkins. What can we do for you?" he asked without extending his hand.

Ms. DeMarco stood up. Nancy DeMarco. Medium build, Harpo hair, and late of the Massachusetts Commission Against Discrimination. Empire had had one of the worst sex-discrimination-in-promotion records in the Northeast, and Ms. DeMarco had been the one who crammed it down our throats. I'd met her once across a crowded conference-room table. Aside from an Empire stenographer, she had been the only woman present. She'd won.

"Mr. Cuddy," she acknowledged. I stopped at a leather chair, and we all sat down together.

"Well," I said, "this doesn't seem to be my day for surprise attacks."

Silence from them.

And from me, too.

Then Perkins: "Why are you here?"

"You must have discovered that in the process of finding out who I am."

"Amateurish, Mr. Cuddy, amateurish. That phone call, I mean."

"Look, Mr. Perkins," I said, "let's stop the urinating contest. Notice I avoided 'pissing' out of respect for your decor. You're one of the best in Boston at what you do. You've been asked to find Stephen Kinnington. So have I. He appears to have run away, so there is probably no criminal element behind the disappearance, and therefore nobody to tipoff. Why don't we share information and coordinate those efforts?"

"Our client does not appreciate your involvement, Mr. Cuddy."

"Does the judge appreciate that every hour we don't find Stephen increases the chances that we won't find him?"

"We will find the boy—and as soon as this conference is over, Ms. DeMarco can resume her efforts in that direction."

I looked over at Ms. DeMarco. She was looking at Perkins without expression.

I rose and sidled toward the door. "Mr. Perkins, I guess I can understand why you don't want to tell me what you know. What I can't understand is why you don't want to find out what I know." I opened the door. "Amateurish, Mr. Perkins, amateurish."

Ninth

I had a drink at Clarke's while I waited for my photos to be finished. They were ready as Danny had promised.

When I arrived at the apartment an hour later, the red light on my tape machine told me I'd had some calls. The first message was from Valerie. The usual you're-a-tough-man-to-reach-but-I-forgive-you. Then there were three dial tones, meaning that whoever had called had hung up instead of leaving a message. Then there was this:

"I don't like leaving messages, even for a discriminating man like you. Meet me at Father's First at eight P.M."

I might have had some question about the voice, but not the "discriminating" tag. I wondered if she'd wear a disguise.

I dialed Mrs. Kinnington's number. Mrs. Page answered, grumbled, and told me to hang on.

"What have you to report?" asked my client.

"Precious little. Everybody but the psychiatrist is slamming doors in my face."

"Does that mean my son is aware of your efforts on my behalf?"

"It does," I said, and I summarized my day for her.

She sounded like a little girl when she spoke again.

"I should have realized that your prediction about his discovering you would be accurate. I am an old woman, Mr. Cuddy, autocratic and perhaps even cranky. Stephen is all I care about anymore. I will pay you to search for him until you advise me it's hopeless."

"I'll call you again when I know more."

"By the way, I was never contacted by this De-Marco girl regarding Stephen."

"That's odd. Maybe she thought it best not to disturb you."

"Perhaps that's what she was told to think."

I was nodding as I hung up. I drummed my fingers on the tape machine, then dialed another number.

Valerie picked it up on the second ring.

"It's John," I said.

"Oh, John, how are you doing? What have you found out?"

"Not too much. I'd like to ask you some questions about Stephen."

"Oh, I'm ten minutes late for a tennis match now, and Marie will have to give up the court if I'm not there in five minutes. How about meeting me for a drink tonight."

"Sorry. Prior engagement."

"Oh." I could hear her frown over the phone.

"I'll be in Bonham early tomorrow morning. How about lunch?"

"Terrific. I'll pack a picnic basket and we can go down to a great swimming beach, and we—"

"Slow down. You're on vacation. I'm working."

The frown-pause again. "Well, you still have to eat lunch, don't you?"

"Yes."

"Good. Pick me up at my place. Seventeen Fordham Road, first floor. Eleven-thirty. I've got to run. Bring your trunks. 'Bye."

"Val—"

Click.

Annoying woman.

Tenth

IF Father's First were located in a poorer neighborhood than Beacon Hill, it would be a dive. Being on Charles Street, it's a charming institution. It's dark, dingy, and jukeboxed, with a mixed bag of gays, MBTA motormen, nursing students from Mass General, and law students from Suffolk University. I spotted her near the corner. She *was* wearing a disguise, sort of.

I slid in next to her. "I like your fatigue jacket," I said.

She looked down into her beer. "You realize that this could cost me a job I've worked toward for six years?"

I ordered a screwdriver. "If it makes you meet guys like me in places like this, it can't be such a great job."

She looked up, but her hands kept toying with her beer mug. "It's not, really." She reached into a big leather tote bag and withdrew a file folder. She passed it to me. "Read it. No notes. No copying."

It took all of three minutes to read.

"This is it?"

"Yup."

"After two weeks?"

She nodded.

"What's going on, Ms. DeMarco?"

"Nancy, please," she said, more I thought from anonymity than cordiality. She took a sip of beer and began. "The case came in through Perkins on the thirteenth, the day after Stephen disappeared. He assigned me right away. He handed me the police reports, which he'd already had copies of. After I read them, he told me I'd be on my own because the judge wanted a quiet, accent *quiet*, investigation."

"How can you find a fourteen-year-old under that kind of mandate?"

"You can't. Look at the file. Initial police report. Five-minute call to the housekeeper. Follow-up police report. Alert calls to airport and train-station security. One leg visit to the bus stations. End present efforts."

"Amateurish."

She grimaced. "Worse. Perkins himself has loaded me with other files. I'm not complaining, but I was the operative with the most files pre-Stephen, and I've gotten more than my share since. Every time I try to do something on Stephen's case, Perkins moves up the priority of some other case I'm on. I'd be embarrassed to talk with the judge—assuming Perkins would let me."

I confirmed that Smollett's signature was on both the initial and follow-up reports before I closed up the file and passed it back to her. "What do you suppose Perkins is trying to tell you?"

She put down her beer. "He's a professional. That

means minimal effort is intentional. And that probably means pressure from the client to keep it that way."

I took a sip of my screwdriver. "You know anything about the judge's wife?"

She looked surprised. "Perkins told me she was dead."

I nodded. "Years ago. It pushed Stephen off the deep end. I was wondering if something similar pushed him again."

She shrugged. "I don't know. But then, what I don't know about this case could make a mini-series."

I smiled sympathetically. "It's not your fault, you know. You're a professional who's being reined in."

"Yeah." She finished her beer and slid off the stool. "If you need to talk to me again, which I hope you don't, call me at the office and identify yourself as Mr. Pembroke but don't leave a return number."

"By the way, why did you decide to call me?" I asked.

She smiled as she slung her bag. "What we're doing stinks. And in the office you didn't refer to him as 'the kid' or 'the boy.' You called him by his name, Stephen. Poor little son of a bitch."

Eleventh

THE next day was bright and clear. There was only one cruiser in the range parking area. Cal was waiting for me inside the wire enclosure. He waved to the short wooden tower, which was centered just inside the range. The tower man buzzed me in through the gate. Bonham may not be a big-budget town, but Chief Calvin Maslyk knew where the money he got was best spent.

"Been a while, John."

"Nearly four weeks."

We picked up some sonic muffs and wad-cutter cartridges and moved to the seventy-five-foot line, just left of center. Cal had already set up some traditional bull's-eyes downrange, one target easel apart. We adjusted the muffs over our ears, and the tower man clicked on.

"Gentlemen, load five rounds." We did so. Then the tower again. "Is there anyone down range?" A pause. Then again. "Is there anyone down range?" Another pause. "The range is clear. Ready on the right. Ready on the left." We waved. "Ready on the firing line." A pause. Then, "Fire."

We fired five rounds, single-shot. "Clear your weapons." We opened our cylinders, jacked out the expended shells, and slid our fingers into the gun frame so the cylinder could not close back in.

"Is the firing line clear?" intoned the tower. We held up our weapons, cylinders out. "The firing line is clear. You may proceed downrange." We began walking toward the targets.

I liked Cal, and I liked the way he required his range to be run. I'd read about a chief on the South Shore who hadn't taken those precautions. A nine-year-old, playing army, had crawled onto the range. A rookie cop who never saw him hit him twice. The boy died the next day, and the rookie resigned the day after. The chief was forced out the following week by the board of selectmen, the governing body of the town.

Usually Cal outscores me. This time he slaughtered me. "Something on your mind, John?"

"Have you got any unbreakable vows toward Meade?"

He measured me evenly. "None past neighborliness."

"I'm trying to find Stephen Kinnington, the judge's son. It looks to me like the judge has told the present searchers to stand down and has sealed the case against outsiders like me."

"Unfortunate family, the Kinningtons."

With a pencil he marked our bullet holes on the targets so we'd know that unmarked holes came from our next shots. We walked back to the firing line.

"Feel like talking about them?" I asked.

He rubbed his chin as we approached the bench. "The judge's brother, Telford, was killed in 'Nam, oh, 1969, maybe. The wife died four or so years ago. Went off the Swan Street bridge into the Concord. I suspect the booze caused the crash."

"No autopsy?" I said as the tower told us to load five more.

"No body."

"In the Concord?" I asked. "That river's current barely pushes a leaf."

The tower man's voice crackled in the background. Cal clicked his cylinder shut. "It was early spring, John. Big from the snows and rain. When they pulled the car up, she wasn't in it. Never found her."

"Was one of the doors open?"

Cal smiled and pulled his muffs on. The tower man finished his liturgy. We fired the second string double-action and again cleared our weapons.

As we moved downrange again, Cal continued the conversation. "Smollett's diver said he didn't notice."

"Did you say 'driver' or 'diver'?"

"Diver, as in scuba diver."

"Meade has its own scuba team?"

"Of sorts. Meade is 'concerned about crime.' At least I think that's Smollett's usual budget speech. Pretty effective speech, too."

"Cal, I'm told that the kid flipped soon after his mother's death. Institutionalized. Then he was apparently fine until two weeks ago. Can you tell me anything about his disappearance?"

Cal frowned and dropped his voice. "Smollett never even called me to put me on alert. I found out from one of my men whose wife works in the cafeteria in Stephen's school. Nothing on the radio or the computer. Nothing at all."

We reached the targets. "Can you think of any reason the judge wouldn't want his son found?"

Cal clucked his tongue, perhaps at the question, but more likely at my miserable shooting. "Maybe the kid just doesn't fit into his system." He began penciling our shots. "The judge, who by the way this department and I have to live with, is a cold, cold man. Just the opposite of his brother, who was real personable, though in an unpredictable sort of way. But the judge . . . well, if you ever saw him in court, you'd know what I mean."

"I have. I've also met his bodyguard."

"Bodyguard? Oh, Blakey?"

I nodded.

"Blakey," said Cal. "He's a bad-ass, John. He was on the Meade PD, then broke up a fight in a tavern a little—no, a lot—too hard. Citzens' group managed to raise enough fuss to get him off the force, because he was still probationary. But then the judge hired him on at the courthouse. One of those political moves that makes the judge look fearless to the law-and-order folks."

Cal pocketed his pencil but made no move back toward the firing line. "You have a jam with him?"

"Sort of," I said.

"Watch his hands, John. He could open coconuts with 'em. By the by, if memory serves, Blakey was the officer who noticed the smashed fencing when Mrs. Kinnington went into the river."

I perked up. "And then sometime later, when Blakey is squeezed off the force, the judge gives him a job?"

Cal nodded.

"How does that add up to you?" I asked.

Cal gave me a philosophical look. "Small-town police chiefs don't add, John; they subtract. Every time they take a stand, they subtract from their support in the town. Support remembers only the times when you do what they *don't* want. Enough subtractions and there's a new chief to do the arithmetic. I don't know what happened between His Honor, Smollett, and Blakey."

While I decided not to push my luck any further, Cal walked over to a locker at the end of the range and came back with a stapler and two bigger cardboard targets. He stapled them onto the target easels. They were full-sized, human silhouettes.

"Why these?" I asked.

"You didn't do real well on those first two strings, John. Never can tell when you might need to be better." We turned and walked back toward the firing line.

"Combat string," he yelled to the tower man.

Twelfth

FORDHAM Road was a short street of older houses three blocks from the center of town. I parked and rang the bell marked *V. Jacobs*.

"Oh, John, I've been leaving messages for you all morning. Where have you been?" She was dressed in a halter top and shorts. Both were pastel and the colors clashed a bit.

"What's the news?"

She ran back down the hall, disappeared, then reappeared with a picnic basket and a beach bag.

"I ran into Miss Pitts this morning in the market. You remember, the retired teacher who had Stephen in the fifth grade? We have to go see her right away."

She was past me and halfway to my car. I shrugged and followed after her.

The living room was filled with the kinds of things one obtains with trading stamps. Plastic-brass floor lamps, plastic-walnut cocktail tables, and plastic Hummel-like sculptures on eight separate knicknack-holding shelf arrangements. My rocking chair, however, was built of massive pine. It must have gone for twelve and a half books, minimum.

Miss Pitts was plump and spoke in a soft purr. The

three of us held teacups and coffee cakes in our hands and on our laps in a precarious balance that I've never been able to master. Miss Pitts had thus far covered her brightest class (1959), and her catlike voice was slowly putting me to sleep. I began to wonder why the hell she had the cocktail tables if she wasn't going to use them for the tea and cakes. I was giving serious consideration to cutting a fart to change the direction of the conversation, when Valerie mercifully jumped first.

"Miss Pitts, what year was it you had Stephen?"

"Ah, Stephen, Stephen. What an unfortunate story. Oh, one of today's wicked novelists would have a field day with his sad life. But the brightest boy, the absolute brightest I've ever seen. No one, not even in the class of nineteen-fifty-nine, could touch him."

"Actually, Miss Pitts," I broke in, setting my cup, saucer, and goodies on the floor, "what I'm interested in is whether anyone *has* touched him. In the unfriendly sense, I mean."

"Uh, quite," said Miss Pitts, a bit miffed, I thought. "Well, as I told Miss Jacobs this morning, two weeks ago, on the twelfth, I was taking my evening exercise. I used to call it my constitutional, but after the way some groups have twisted one meaning of that word, I have ceased to use it at all. In any case, while I was walking down Ballard Street, I saw Stephen ahead of me, carrying his books. No doubt he was so late in heading home—it was nearly five-thirty, you see— because he had visited the library after school. Well, seeing him I was about to call to him, when a black sedan screeched to a halt on the street beside him. He took one look at the driver and was gone."

"Did the driver go after him?" I asked.

"Hah, not likely. Stephen is as springy and quick as an antelope. That Gerry Blakey couldn't have caught him on horseback, assuming a horse could bear him any better than this town can."

"What happened then?"

"Well, Blakey, who'd gotten half out of the driver's side, muttered something, slid back in, and drove off."

I leaned back. Miss Pitts's eyes might be getting a little weak, but she wouldn't be likely to mistake Stephen, and no one could mistake Blakey.

"Why didn't you report this to the police?" I asked.

She gave me a sour look. "The police? Hmph. Will Smollett is a fool who can't even control the teenage hoodlums in this town, much less be its chief investigative officer. Besides, he's in the judge's pocket. Everyone knows that. And if Blakey was chasing Stephen, the judge was likely connected with Stephen's leaving. That's why I decided to tell Eleanor."

"You mean Valerie."

She determinedly set down her teacup and rose. "Young man, you are smug, and you are rude. If I were to say 'Valerie' I would mean Miss Jacobs. When I say 'Eleanor,' I mean Eleanor Kinnington. I'm afraid this interview is over."

I glanced to my right. Valerie seemed as stunned at the reference to Mrs. Kinnington as I was.

I stood politely and looked at our hostess. "Miss Pitts, please accept my apology. I *was* rude, and I assumed you were a meandering old woman who might confuse things. I was wrong. But I've been retained to try to find a probably terrified fourteen-year-old child, and you're the first bright spot I've come across. Can we please talk a while longer?"

Miss Pitts's face softened, and she sat back down. "He is such a dear, dear boy."

We covered the intersections of Miss Pitts's and Stephen's lives during the prior six months. Nothing was produced that sounded helpful. I decided that a quiet interlude was appropriate before we moved back to tougher ground.

"What can you tell me about Telford Kinnington, the judge's brother?"

Miss Pitts gave a bittersweet smile. "Ah, Telford Kinnington. He was three years younger than the judge, and enough unlike him to have been bought from the Gypsies. The judge, who went to public school here too, was a plodder. Everything seemed to come easily to Telford, though. A gifted student, a fine athlete at Harvard, and a true patriot, Mr. Cuddy. Telford didn't just talk about this country, he died fighting for it. Only a few months after he'd been home on leave, too. In fact, I still have the newspaper account of his last battle. Just a minute."

She bustled over to a stuffed bookcase and levered out a scrapbook. I feared a lengthy, unproductive tangent coming on. I thought about telling her to forget it but decided I was talking to her on borrowed time as it was.

"Let me see," she said, turning pages with agonizing slowness. "Yes, yes, here it is." She passed me the open book.

There were two accounts, one from the *Banner*, a local paper, and one from the *Globe*. Both were dated April 11, 1969. According to the local paper, Captain Telford Kinnington had led his company in a counterattack from an American position against a much larger Vietcong force that was engaging a separate sector of the position. He and nearly a quarter of his company (about 40 of 160) were killed or wounded, but the VC had been annihilated. The medal he'd received, however, was, in my experience, not a very substantial award for a heroic charge.

The *Globe* article, written a bit more tongue in cheek, implied ever so gently that his action had been unnecessary and reckless. It also indicated that he'd entered the service as a second lieutenant five years earlier and had only recently been promoted to captain—a long time to wait for his second bar in those casualty-ridden late sixties. I noted the part of the war zone involved and remembered that I knew someone from Intelligence who'd served there after I'd come home.

I then swung the conversation as delicately as I could back to the judge's late wife. Miss Pitts was reluctant at first, but once I emphasized the importance of my knowing Stephen's earlier life, our hostess lapsed into the nearly universal enthusiasm with which people discuss those who appear big but turn out to be little.

"Diane Kinnington was a terror, Mr. Cuddy, a demon from hell. The judge met her when he was in law school. At first she was an enchanting girl, and I served with her on several town committees just after their marriage. Diane continued to be active in town matters far into her pregnancy with Stephen. But for a while before he was born, she began acting . . . well, strange. She appeared at committee meetings with alcohol on her breath. She walked past people she knew on the street as though she never saw them. She began wearing sunglasses even into the evening, and despite two servants at the big house, she sometimes slipped into Carver's, the small grocery store in Meade Center, to buy odd items. Then one September night something happened. I've never talked with anybody who knew just what. But Diane was hospitalized, and Stephen was born a few hours later, two months premature."

"Miss Pitts, can you tell me who would know what happened that night?"

She frowned. "Yes, for all the good it would do. Her obstetrician couldn't be reached in time, and Dr. Ketchum, who was the family's doctor, rushed down and delivered her of Stephen. He wouldn't talk about it, and he died a few months later. Both servants, a woman and her husband, were let go within a week, I suspected because they were supposed to be keeping an eye on her and somehow failed. They headed south somewhere. No one else that I know of was involved."

"How did she get to the doctor's office?"

"Her husband."

"But surely, if she was hospitalized, there'd be records of what her trouble was."

"Oh, she was hospitalized, all right, but in a private place, if you get me."

"A sanatorium?" I decided to use the "old parlance."

"Yes, out in the Berkshires."

Coincidence? "Does the name Willow Wood ring any bells?"

"What?"

"The name Willow Wood. Was that the sanatorium Diane Kinnington was in?"

She shook her head. "I don't know. I think it was the same one Stephen stayed in."

69

"What do you know about the night Diane died?"

She sighed. "Even less, I'm afraid. Just the newspaper stories, and I didn't keep them. After Stephen was born, Diane seemed to . . . well, rally back in spirit. Then, a few years later, she began to decline again. By the time Stephen reached my class, she had declined frighteningly. If her earlier conduct was strange, her later behavior was wicked. Drunkenness, rowdiness, and . . . well . . . "

"Miss Pitts, I know this must be difficult—"

"Oh, you know nothing, young man, nothing!" she snapped. "You know I'm relatively old and therefore you 'know' that I'm patriotic and narrow-minded and a prude. Well, we may have felt strongly about some things when I was young, like love of country and order and respect. But maybe we felt differently about other things than you think we did. And maybe while we didn't go around talking about things, we nevertheless knew how to enjoy ourselves. But what we didn't do was what she did with every male that she could."

"Message received and understood, Miss Pitts," I said. She calmed down a bit, and Valerie gave me an approving smile. "What about Stephen thereafter?"

She sighed again. "He'd been so obviously affected by his mother's behavior. He had become erratic in school, and then his mother showed up roaring drunk for a student-teacher conference, with a . . . a man waiting for her in the car. Well, things must have been twice as bad at home. The day after Diane's accident, the judge whisked Stephen away to the sanatorium. The school records don't show it, but I'm sure that poor boy suffered a complete nervous breakdown. He returned to school the next year. He had lost a year, but he seemed to be doing so well until now."

"Do you remember anything else that might help us?" I asked.

"I'm afraid not. Although . . . "

"Yes?" prompted Valerie.

"Well," she looked from Valerie to me, "there was a reporter named Thomas Doucette on the *Banner* at the time Diane died. The rumor was that he'd been assigned to the story and, well, covered it a little too well. Anyway, no article by him appeared in the paper, and he quit the *Banner* a few weeks later, though most people figured he was fired. Just as well actually. He was the least gifted boy in the class of '61, and certainly not destined for the Pulitzer Prize."

"Does he still live in Meade?" I asked.

"No. No, he lives somewhere in Boston now. At least that's what I remember from his uncle's funeral, and that was, oh, two years ago. You might try his parents, though. They're retired, too, and live on Moody Street."

I had run out of topics, so I decided there was nothing to be lost by asking what was on my mind.

"One last thing, Miss Pitts. What did Eleanor Kinnington say when you told her about seeing Blakey with Stephen?"

Miss Pitts, to my great surprise, blushed and her look saddened. "Well, what could she say? She said she had suspected as much but had hoped against hope that she was wrong."

"Wrong about what?"

Miss Pitts suddenly stabbed several times at a box of tissues on the table next to her.

"Gerald Blakey is thirty years old and has never

71

been seen in this town in the company of a woman, Mr. Cuddy. Isn't that enough to be wrong about?"

She hurried from the room, crying.

Thirteenth

"I guess you don't feel like a picnic anymore, do you?"

We were back in the car, and Valerie's were the first words spoken since we'd left Miss Pitts.

"Actually, I'd love a picnic," I said. She smiled broadly. "As long as the conversation level is low enough to give me some time to sort things out."

"Terrific!" she said, and shook her hair down onto her shoulders.

"But first," I said, "let's be sure we can reach this Thomas Doucette character, class of '61."

We stopped at a gas station and I called Boston information. No Thomas Doucette nor T. Doucette. Then I tried the elder Doucettes. Again, no listing in Meade. We decided to stop at Moody Street and see the Doucettes on the way to the beach.

Valerie directed me up and down and left and right through semi-rural, increasingly narrow roads. If there was a poorer section of Meade, this was it. We pulled onto Moody Street and up to a small and old, but neatly kept, ranch house to which someone had added a little greenhouse. The mailbox had "Doucette" in paste-on letters. There were three or four similar homes on the street, but no sense of development or planning. It was as though the distance between houses was less a function of privacy or exclusivity and more a reaction to the undesirability of the intervening and uneven scrub-pine land.

A small, four-door American subcompact sat in the driveway, and a small woman stood at the screen door. We left our car and started up the path toward her.

She had been watching us leave the car and approach her. She stepped outside and looked around. She had light blue hair and a troubled expression. "May I help you?"

"Yes," said Valerie. "Are you Mrs. Doucette?"

"Yes."

"Mrs. Doucette, I'm Valerie Jacobs. I teach eighth grade at the Lincoln Drive School. This is a friend of mine, John Cuddy. We'd like to contact your son Thomas."

By the time Valerie had finished, we were nearly to her. At the mention of Thomas, Mrs. Doucette stiffened and eyed us both very carefully.

"Thomas doesn't live here anymore," she said carefully.

"We know," I said.

"He also likes his privacy," she continued.

"And he's entitled to enjoy it," I said.

Before I could continue, Valerie broke in. "Mrs. Doucette, we simply need to speak with him about a news story he covered years ago. A young boy's safety is at stake."

Mrs. Doucette's eyebrows shot up. "The Kinnington boy?"

"That's right," said Valerie, flashing her most ingratiating smile.

"Goddamn him!" Mrs. Doucette bit off her words. "Goddamn him and his whole family!" She stormed into the house, slamming the screen door behind her. She whirled. "And you! Goddamn you for reminding me of them!" She slammed the inner door.

"What the . . ." began Valerie.

"Face it, Val. You blew it. You're just not cut out for this kind of work."

I was back in the car and had it started by the time a frowning, frustrated Valerie tired of knocking at the Doucettes' door and began walking down to me.

Valerie had gotten over my teasing by the time we reached the parking lot of the swimming beach. We respectively entered a rustic, large cabin, "Men" on one side and "Women" on the other.

Coming out of the women's side of the locker building, Val's legs looked a little thicker than they had in the other outfits I'd seen her wear to date. The rest of her looked triple A, however. I got a slight flush when she flickered an appraising eye over my new physique. This was the first time I'd worn a pair of trunks in quite a while, and I decided I liked sporting the results my conditioning had produced. We walked toward the water.

The long, manmade swimming beach edged into trees and picnic tables at one end and into a parking lot at the other. The beach was nearly empty, most people being under the trees at the tables. Owning no sandals, I toughed out the blistering sand in bare feet. We finally pitched our blanket at what looked like a quiet spot about fifty feet to the left of a perfectly tanned elderly couple sitting and reading in half-legged sand chairs.

We talked around Mrs. Kinnington for a while before I brought her up.

"You know, Val, I'm on the verge of leaving this case."

Her face was stricken. "Oh, please, John—please don't!"

I rearranged my legs Indian-style on the blanket. "Look, I won't be violating any confidence by telling you that my client did not mention word one about Miss Pitts and the scene with Stephen and Blakey. That could be an important link in the chain of Stephen's disappearance, and if Mrs. Kinnington knew about it, she should have told me."

She faked casualness by stretching out on her stomach, longways to the just-past-zenith sun. "Is the reason he left really that important to your finding him?"

I leaned back. "Possibly, yes; probably not, if he's gone voluntarily."

"But Mrs. Kinnington said she told you that the things he took were only things he'd know to take."

I closed my eyes. "Yeah, but that suggests only that he voluntarily decided to leave. It doesn't go far in suggesting what might have happened twenty feet from his back door."

She came up to her knees with a start. "Do you really believe something happened to him?"

"That's just the problem, Val. I'm not being helped by anybody in this case, or even permitted to gather the facts I could use to reach a decision like that."

She put her hand on my right forearm and

squeezed, a little too long and a little too hard. "John, you know that—"

The moment was broken by a loud and worthy curse from the elderly man next to us. Three boyish bruisers, built like college football players, were laughing at him and his wife. He rose from his chair and shook a book-clutching fist at a sign I could barely read while he and his wife brushed sand off themselves.

"The goddamned sign says no goddamned ball playing on the beach!" he yelled.

The biggest of the three, cradling the ball professionally in the crook of his arm, replied, "Fuck you."

"We'll get the cops!" yelled the old man.

"And the lifeguard!" yelled the old woman.

"The fuckin' cops are off drinking and the fuckin' lifeguard knows I'll kick his ass if he lets his shadow fall on me." The other kids laughed, and they continued their running and passing drills up the beach. The big boy had the right moves; the other two were barely adequate. The old man sat down sputtering.

"Nice kid," I said to Val.

"Craig Mann," she said disgustedly. "His father's a selectman, so nobody will do anything about him. He was a real high school star, tight end, I think. Last fall the local paper was full of his gridiron heroics at U Mass/Amherst."

"Why wouldn't the local paper have been full of Stephen's disappearance?"

She frowned. "Judge Kinnington probably owns most of it."

I leaned back down. "A few more questions, then some fuel and reflection," I said. I felt her settle her bottom on the blanket like a witness on the stand. I also felt a stirring in my trunks that I hadn't expected.

"Did you ever have reason to believe that Stephen was involved with Blakey in any way, with or without consent?"

"No. I mean Stephen is not exactly average, but he's not abnormal. At least, not that way. I don't mean I think that . . .that *that* is abnormal, you know, if that's what an adult, two adults, I mean, decide to do, but . . . "

"Okay. Assuming Stephen left involuntarily, he could have been taken to a place none of us would ever guess or stumble on. So let's assume that Stephen's on his own. We don't know where he went, but we have to start somewhere. So how would he get where he's going?"

"Hitchhiking," said Val as she squeaked open the Styrofoam chest. "John, I'm sorry, but I'm starving. Can we start just a little bit early?" I didn't like her voice when it wheedled.

"Yes, we can start," I said, "but hitchhiking, at least toward his destination, isn't likely. He's smart enough to fear he'd be remembered and recognized. He might have hitchhiked *away* from here, though, and toward some other form of transportation."

"Like a bus station?" She unwrinkled some aluminum foil.

"Good thought, but they've been checked, apparently competently." I sat up.

Val said, "Just let me toss these away so they won't blow, and then we can dig in." She trotted off with some paper toward a trash basket. I noticed that the Dallas Cowboys were headed back toward us. As they approached Valerie, Big Boy made some remark that sounded like, "Hey, hey, school is *out*, boys." Val shook her head and trotted back to the blanket. The boys whooped a little at her distinctly feminine gait.

"I just so hate people like that," she said as she reached into the cooler.

"Can you think of any type of transportation Stephen might try to use?" I asked.

She cut a hunk of cheese and passed it and some gourmet crackers over to me. I reached over and poured the wine. I had my head down as she answered. "No, not really. Of course, he—Hey!"

I looked up to catch part of a rooster-tail of sand in my wine and all over the cheese.

"Sorry, lovers, but that pass was in the fourth quarter, and we needed it to keep our drive alive," said Big Boy over his shoulder as he loped away from us.

I raised my voice so it would crack. "You fellows ought to have some respect for others, you know."

"Oh, I have lots of respect for Miss Jacobs, pop," he yelled, his pals hooting. I noticed Big Boy was wearing jean cut-offs held up by an old belt. Off to our right, the old man was sputtering again.

Val was looking at me oddly, the way you react when someone you've so far liked shows some weakness or failing, like dropping a racist remark.

"Sorry about the cheese," I said as I brushed it off.

"Oh, that's okay, John," she said uncertainly, dropping her eyes a little and fussing with the crackers.

"By the way," I said, "do you have a hairbrush in that bag of yours?"

She looked up. "A what?"

"A hairbrush."

She turned awkwardly for it without taking her eyes off me. "Yes, yes I do." She dipped into her bag and produced a big blue plastic one with a thick handle and a broad working end.

"Thanks," I said, and slid it between two folds in the blanket. "Now, can you think of any form of transportation Stephen might favor?"

She tried to refocus her thoughts. "No. No."

I heard some thudding behind me and, sure enough, my imitation of the all-American wimp was drawing the all-American schmuck inexorably back toward us. He did a stop-and-go turnaround, which again showered the elderly couple. He then came chugging at us full tilt, following the wobbly arc of the ball, his face turned back over his shoulder.

Val, believing, reasonably, that she had to try to take charge of the situation, rolled up onto her knees and yelled, "Hey, watch out!"

Big Boy did nothing to show that he heard her. He was about twenty feet from us. I figured he would glance once at us to orient himself and then plant his left leg, the one closest to us, just outside our blanket in order to (1) turn sharply to receive the pass and (2) inundate us with another tidal wave of sand. I waited and then did what every schoolyard kid knows how to do.

I stuck out my foot.

Big Boy's left foot landed just before my outstretched calf. As he pivoted on that foot to redirect his momentum, the sand flew all over me. As he stepped off, though, my lower leg was a bar to his left leg, and he toppled. He hit the sand heavily on his left shoulder, with the awkwardness and impact that you see only when an athlete who knows how to fall from combat goes down because of an accidental shot from his teammate. He also missed the pass.

I was standing a count before he was. I hoped that what I'd done would so embarrass him that he'd think only a punch could avenge him. He came up spitting sand and obscenities. He wound up with his right fist and let fly at my head. I parried it with my left, slashing the edge of my hand into his forearm. As I slashed, I cocked my right hand, fingers outstretched but slightly cupped to avoid jamming them, and then drove it up and into his solar plexis. There was a noise from his mouth like the sudden flapping of a sail that's lost its wind and purpose. He sank to one knee and started to gag. I dropped to one knee, reached back for the hairbrush, and then yanked him by his hair over my other leg. I spanked him hard and loud with the hairbrush. He had about enough air to go "Emphh!" on each swat and wriggle a little.

After about ten strokes, my palm was beginning to ring, the way it feels if you catch a hardball in the wrong part of the glove. I tossed the hairbrush onto the blanket and looked around for his friends. They were transfixed about twenty feet away. I rolled Big Boy off my leg and stood up. I reached down, gripped his belt dead center at the small of his back, and lifted him like a four-limbed suitcase. It's really pretty easy to do, even with a heavy man, since you are able to lift him at an almost perfect balance point, but it's impressive as hell. I then walked purposefully down into the water until I was at mid-thigh. I yo-yoed him five times into the water to help focus the sting the spanking imparted. He was making little gurgling sounds. I carried him back up the beach and stopped in front of his friends. I dropped him like a sack of battered junk.

"And if you do this again," I said to them, shaking my index finger, "you're all going to bed without any supper."

As I returned to our blanket, the elderly man caught

up with me. He was grinning and hopping from one foot to the other. He started pumping my hand.

"Boy, oh boy, son, that's the best show I've seen since the war! That miserable bastard's been terrorizing this beach for years. My name's Graden. Charlie Graden. If you need anybody to stand up for you with the cops or anything, you call me, me and Edna. We're in the book. Boy, oh boy!"

I smiled at him. "Thanks, Mr. Graden. If this were twenty years ago, I'll bet *I'd* be the one shaking *your* hand."

"Damn right!" he said, giggling. "Take care of yourself, son." He trotted, only a little uncertainly, back toward his chair.

When I reached the blanket, Val had already packed everything back in the chest and had her tank top on.

I said, "We can stop for lunch . . ."

She glared up at me with tears in her eyes. "You're just as bad as they are, you know. Only you don't know it. You could have handled that boy easily, any time you wanted. You used that whiny voice to encourage him to come back." Now her voice cracked with emotion. "I thought you were a sincere, caring guy looking for a poor little boy. But all you are is a showoff too, just like those college kids. The only difference is, your shows are a little more clever and a lot more violent." She picked up her cooler with one hand, yanked up her blanket with the other, and strode determinedly off, trying unsuccessfully to gather the sand-trailing blanket into a bundle with just one hand.

As I picked up my keys and shook out my towel, it seemed that her version edged closer to the mark than

81

the old man's and mine did. I spent most of the drive back to Boston trying to persuade myself the other way.

Fourteenth

I stopped at the apartment to shower. While I was drying off, I found the telephone number of one of the two contacts I planned to speak to that afternoon.

Dave Waters and I had been first lieutenants together in Saigon in 1968. He absorbed a lot of indirect abuse during his first week until the day that a good ol' boy told him to shag his black ass after some coffee. About ten minutes later Dave began absorbing a lot of direct respect. The good ol' boy told the doctors he'd been hit by a Renault.

The last number I had for Dave was with the Denver P.D. I tried it.

"Lieutenant Waters' line," answered the voice.

"May I speak to him, please? Tell him it's Lieutenant John Cuddy."

"Hold on, sir." A pause.

"Waters here."

"Still a lieutenant, I see."

"Christ, I was afraid it was you," his voice becoming jocular. "You still padding insurance claims?"

"No, but that's a long story. I'm on my own now,

and I need some information about a war hero in 'Nam."

"I didn't know anybody recognized heroes anymore."

"This was in your sector, your second tour, April of sixty-nine. A captain named Telford Kinnington led a charge from a protected position against some VC attackers. Remember it?"

A sigh at the other end. "Jesus, I'll never forget it. When I read the initial field report, I was scared stiff that old Telford was one of my persuasion. So I checked the reports and his file myself. He wasn't, but a lot of the cooks and drivers he got the asses shot off were."

"What happened?"

"Kinnington was a wild man. He'd been back in Hawaii a couple of times for battle fatigue. Only he'd never been in battle. He was in intelligence and had spent a tour in Saigon as a lieutenant. Wasn't promoted because, though his two-oh-one file didn't say so, he was damned near a psycho. Even so, he was from some big-time family up by you, so the pressure was put on to promote him. They did, and somehow he wrangled a staff position in a base camp."

"A staff position?"

"Yeah. Some sort of special-liaison crap. One day, while the infantry troops were out on a search and destroy, a 'copter spotted a concentration of VC approaching the camp. The gunships were a little too far away, so the base commander put his only remaining line troops at the points where Charlie was most likely to hit. He put Kinnington with the bakers and candlestick makers at the best natural-barrier side of the camp with sort of ambiguous orders to fend off the attack. It was the ambiguity that saved Telford's memory if not his ass, because when the VC hit the camp at the expected place, Kinnington jumps up and leads his 'company' on a charge at Charlie's flank. Just then the gunships arrive and maul the VC and Kinnington's commandos. The son of a bitch got thirty-some killed and wounded, mostly by 'copter fire.''

"How the fuck did he get a medal then?"

A derisive chuckle at the other end. "How the fuck do you think, John? The family's friends applied pressure. The ambiguity was emphasized and the 'copter killing was excused, and old Telford got himself commended."

"Dave, I appreciate your time. You coming back this way in the near future?"

Another chuckle but different this time. "Thanks anyway, but if my kids are gonna ride buses, I'd sooner they be in Denver than Boston."

"I wish I could disagree with you. See you, Dave."

"'Bye, John."

I hesitated to call Val, because I wanted to catch my other contact before his cocktail hour, which probably began when most people were finishing lunch. But during the drive back to Boston, I had thought of more than my bully-whipping on the beach.

"Hullo," she answered huskily.

"Val, it's John."

"Oh, um . . ."

"Val, please don't hang up."

Quietly she said, "I won't," and sniffled. I was fairly certain she hadn't developed a cold in the last two hours.

We simultaneously said, "I'm sorry," and laughed.

I stopped sooner than she did. "Oh, John," she said finally, "I'm so sorry I acted that way at the beach. It's just that violence, in any form . . . well, it makes me feel sick, and . . ."

"It's all right. After I thought about it, I agreed with you. It's just the way I am. Let's forget it. Okay?"

A final sniffle at the other end of the line. "Okay," she said.

"Val, I've been thinking. Stephen doesn't seem to have confided anything to his family. Was there anybody in his class he was friendly with?"

She paused before answering. "Gee, John, that's a tough one. Like I told you at L'Espalier, he really is different from other kids his age. I never noticed that he palled around with any of the other boys."

"How about the girls?"

Valerie chuckled. "I'm not sure he was feeling the urge yet, although after what Miss Pitts said . . . Hey, wait a minute. There was one girl in the class who kind of, well, looked him over, if you know what I mean."

Boy, did I. "What's her name?"

"Kim Sturdevant. I'm not sure, but I think I remember seeing them eating lunch together when I was on cafeteria duty."

"Can you fix it for me to talk with her?"

"I don't know," she replied. "I've met her mother at parent-teacher conferences. Kind of mousy but okay. Her father I haven't met, but I have the impression he runs kind of a tight ship."

"Maybe if you called the mother and sweet-talked her . . ."

"I'm not so sure my sweet-talking is very effective anymore."

I let Val's oblique comment pass and pressed about

Kim. "Val, I don't see any other way for us to get inside Stephen's thoughts."

"Well," sighing, "I'll give it a try. Call me—no, I'll call you to let you know how I made out."

"Right. 'Bye and thanks."

"Why not show your thanks?"

"How?" I said before thinking.

"Dinner!" she whooped. "But at my place, since you treated at L'Espalier and since the picnic was, well, . . ."

I thought about Val, and then I thought about Beth. "I don't think I can make it."

"Oh, the men of your generation are so backward about accepting dates. I'm having supper with a friend from college in Boston tomorrow night anyway. How about Saturday?"

"Val, I don't know how the case will be—"

"Like I said about the picnic, you still have to eat. See you here at seven. I'll even provide the wine."

"Val—"

Click.

That was twice.

"I'm tired, John. Dog-tired, damned-tired, down-and-out tired."

I let him unwind for a couple of reasons. First, we were in his office. Second, in my opinion, Mo (for Morris) Katzen at age fifty-three is the best reporter in Boston. He is also the only reporter on the *Herald American* who will speak to me, and I don't know anybody on the *Globe*. Since there are only two major newspapers in Boston, and since I was trying to locate a reporter or ex-reporter, I needed to talk to Mo. So I let him unwind awhile.

"I'm tired of sports. I'm tired of the Red Sox breakin' our hearts, I'm tired of the Patriots not even breakin' our hearts. I'm tired of prizefights in hockey games and ballet dancing in prizefights."

"Sports can be frustrating, Mo," I said.

"Tell me about it." Mo paused to puff obscenely on a cigar that looked as fit for a human mouth as a wolf's turd. He had a dour face and so much white wavy hair that at first you thought it was a toupee.

Mo was wearing his uniform: a gray suit with a too-wide tie, visible because he wasn't wearing the coat and the vest was completely unbuttoned. I once asked Mo why he wore that suit. He said it made him look like a lawyer, which made it easier for him to get past screeners of all kinds. Since in twelve years I had seen neither the vest buttoned nor the jacket, period, I had to reserve judgment.

"Tell you what else I'm sick of. Politics. We got a mayor who builds buildings instead of neighborhoods. We got a school committee run by a Federal judge and school kids who can't read and write English. And we got two fuckin' newspapers that don't do anything about it because one's a black-and-white version of *Sports Illustrated* and the other's a gossip rag with one foot in the fiscal grave."

"Politics stinks, Mo," I said, and then, to be sure I wasn't being deficient in my commentary, I added, "And the newspaper business isn't like it used to be."

"Tell me about it." Four more puffs. "At least," two more puffs, "at least in the old days, we covered stories. Aw, people got bought, sure, then as now, but it was more, I dunno, more understandable somehow. People were selling out so their kids could have food or operations, and the stories were good because they'd hurt you, you know. You'd write the story and proof it and say, 'You know, that gets to me, what that poor shit must have been goin' through and now what's gonna happen to him! And you'd read it, you'd read the story in the evening edition and you'd say, 'Jesus, that coulda been me, I learned something today.' "

"I remember those stories, Mo."

"Sure you do. Everybody does." Three puffs. "Everybody old enough anyway. Nowadays, look around, what do you see?"

I looked around. All I saw was Mo's office, which could have passed for Hitler's bunker or a hazardous waste dump.

I looked back at him without an answer. "Youth!" he boomed, coming forward in his chair. "Youth!"

"Youth is everywhere, Mo," I said, nodding my head.

"Damn right. These kids, the kids that the school committee doesn't educate, they graduate from high school anyway. Half of 'em never wrote a book report. Shit, half of those probably never *read* a book. They intern here—'intern,' that's the word they use nowadays for office boy, although both boys and girls can be office boys and you sure as shit better call then men and women or interns for neutral—they intern here because they saw the movie *All the President's Men* a couple of years ago and they wanna be 'journalists.' You hear that, 'journalists.' I haven't met one yet, not one, that's read the *book All the President's Men*, and only two could spell Bernstein's and Woodward's last names right the first time."

"Youth can be sloppy, Mo."

"Aw, it's not just sloppy, it's the way they've been

brought up. On TV and now videogames. Videogames, can you imagine? I got a niece, she can't speak a word of Hebrew. When I was growing up in Chelsea in the late thirties, it was maybe seventy-five percent Jewish, twenty-five percent Italian. All the Jewish kids could speak enough Italian to be polite to the old store owners and whatever, and understand the dirty jokes. The same for the Italian kids with Yiddish and Hebrew. Now, Jesus, we don't even give them names you can recognize any more. That niece of mine is Jennifer. *Jennifer*, can you fucking imagine! When we grew up it was Morris, and Mario, and Patrick. Now it's fucking Jennifer, and Scott, and . . ."

" . . . and Stephen," I said.

"What?"

"And Stephen. With a 'ph' instead of a 'v'."

"Oh, yeah and Stephen, right. Oh, I'm telling you, John, I'm tired, dog-tired, down-and-fucking-out tired."

I glanced down at my watch. Mo usually runs his course in fifteen minutes. and the repetition of his opening stanza is *usually* the giveaway. "Mo, I was wondering . . ."

"You know, that's why they got me in here."

Usually, but not always.

"They gave me my own office. Me, a reporter. No Pulitzer putzin' Prize or anything. Just me. In my day I don't think the city editor had his own office. But I got one. You know why?"

I cleared my throat. "Ah, no, Mo, I don't."

"It's because of them." He swung his hand in an all-inclusive circle. "It's because of youth. The brass is afraid I'll infect them. So they stay out there with their video terminals and I stay in here with my Remington," which he paused to slap firmly but affectionately. "I type my stories on this, then they gotta go to somebody on one of those terminals to be entered. 'Entered.' That's another one of those words like intern."

"Bad words, Mo. One and all."

"Tell me about it. I haven't had three stories in a year get printed without 'constituency' becoming 'constitutional' or 'receive' becoming 'recieve' or . . . oh, I dunno. I'm just so tired. So fuckin' tired."

He paused again to try to resuscitate the cigar. I leaped in.

"Mo, I was wondering if you could help me."

"Sure thing, John." Two puffs. "What's up?"

"I'm trying to locate a guy who was a reporter for a suburban paper and who now is supposed to be in Boston. His name is Thomas Doucette—"

Mo held up his hand to stop me. "He's an assistant editor at the *Gay News* in the South End. I forget the street."

"Thanks, Mo," I said, getting up.

"Hell, if that's all you wanted," he said between puffs, "why didn't you just say so?"

Fifteenth

I had a filling meal at Dante's, a restaurant on Beacon Hill with a spicy Italian menu and an incongruously

Asian staff. It's a candlelit place, spread over several rooms, with low ceilings and fireplaces. I was the only one eating alone. Romantic couples occasionally glanced sympathetically at me as I chomped my linguini and read my *Evening Globe*.

The next morning I started out running four miles but cut it back to two because of the heat. I cleaned up and grabbed a few doughnuts on my way to the rent-a-car, happily still parked where I had left it.

The *Gay News* was located on a South End street that was "in transition." In some cities, that expression is an unfortunate euphemism for a racial evolution. In Boston, however, the expression is used to reflect a building-by-building renovation. The South End (not to be confused with the heavily Irish South Boston, where I grew up) is predominantly narrow streets, some with imitation gas lamps. The architecture is three- and four-story attached brick townhouses, many with beautiful bowfront windows. The population is a mixture of upper middle class, young professionals, gays, blacks, Greeks, Cubans, and a dozen other racial or ethnic minorities. The major condominium developers moved from Back Bay and Beacon Hill to the waterfront, somewhat leap-frogging the South End because of its streetside drug trade and derelicts that are somehow never brought under control. Accordingly, each block is torn between gentrification and degeneration.

The newspaper offices were over a Greek restaurant in the middle of one block. I found a parking space and trudged sweatily up the stairs.

There was no air-conditioning, but by the bustle of activity in the one large cavern you'd never guess that the staff was troubled by the heat. About ten men and two women were telephoning, typing (old Standards, most not even electric), editing, or jabbering cross-desk or cross-room.

A man about twenty-five came up to me. "Can I help you?" he said without expression.

I decided to try a smile. "Mo Katzen at the *Herald* said I might find Thomas Doucette here."

He smiled back. "I'll get him for you." Apparently trading on the news fraternity does open doors.

I watched him walk to the back of the newsroom. He tapped a thirtyish, slim man with short-cropped blond hair who was bent over a spread of papers. My emissary pointed me out, and the blond man nodded and came over, hand extended.

"I'm Thom Doucette. T-H-O-M if you're from the *Herald*, too."

I wasn't sure if Doucette's remark was an inside joke or an acknowledgment of the staff spelling capacity of which Mo had complained. I laughed politely and shook hands.

"My name is John Cuddy. Mo thought you might be able to help me with a story I'm following up."

"Happy to if I can. Mo sat at my table at the last Boston Press luncheon." Doucette gave a quick frown. "He was one of two who would."

I nodded. "It's kind of confidential." I glanced quickly around the room. "Is there some place private we could talk?"

Doucette regarded me for a moment, then said, "Let me make a call first." He turned and moved to a vacant phone. His call was quickly concluded and he came back smiling. "All set. There's a park two blocks from here. It's not private, but it'll be a hell of a lot quieter and probably cooler than this place." He moved past me toward the door.

"That's probably the least amount of time Mo's ever been on the phone in his life. What's your secret?"

Doucette turned and gave me a sly smile. "Mo did say you were a pretty good detective."

The "park" was in a traffic triangle perhaps fifty feet on a side. There were nine newly planted trees and four newly painted benches. One other bench was occupied by two men, one of whom smiled at me while the other frowned at him.

Doucette and I took the farthest bench. There was very little traffic, and a robin played king of the hill to three sparrows in "our" tree. We had bought lemonades at a corner grocery and had just exhausted the subject of Mo Katzen as we settled onto our bench.

"So," said Doucette as he downed the last of his drink, "what's the story you're following?"

"The death of Diane Kinnington. I'm investigating the disappearance of her son, Stephen, and . . ."

I stopped because Doucette's face had turned the color of dry putty, and I was afraid he was about to blow his lemonade all over me.

"Shit," he said, "you're the guy who was at my parents' house."

"That's right. Your mother seemed pretty upset."

"She said it was a man and a woman. But she said they were from the school department."

"No one misrepresented anything," I said quickly. "The woman I was with *is* a schoolteacher. Stephen was one of her students this year. I'm afraid your mother never let me introduce myself."

Doucette gave a short laugh, and some of his color began to return. "That's like Mom. Always protective.

Even to the point of getting the facts wrong."

I sat back on the bench. "What are the facts, Mr. Doucette?"

"Thom, please."

"Thom."

He stared at the ground and licked his lips. "Did the judge hire you?"

Easily answered, but I decided a fuller explanation might advance me. "No. Confidentially, Stephen's grandmother, through that schoolteacher, hired me. So far as I can tell, the judge is hindering, rather than advancing, the search."

Doucette grunted. "That doesn't surprise me." He licked his lips again, looked up at me, and took a deep breath. "Look, moving to Boston and working on this paper, the *Gay News* I mean, has been the best thing in my life. I've pretty much put Meade behind me. If . . . things got opened up again, I can't be part of it."

"I understand."

"No, no, I don't think you do." He seemed to puff up a little, regaining most of his color. "Working on this paper, you get cursed at and jeered at *and* threatened, but small-time stuff. Over the paper's telephone, sometimes at home. That's why I'm unlisted. But, the Kinnington death, that was the real thing. If he . . . if it's found out that I've talked to you, I could be killed. No joke. That was the threat then."

I held him with with my best steady look. "Thom, I promise that I will not tell anyone at any time that I've spoken with you."

Doucette nodded once and swallowed twice. I offered him the rest of my lemonade and he downed it. He cleared his throat. "What do you want to know?"

"As I started to say, I think there's a connection between Diane Kinnington's death and Stephen's disappearance. I don't know what the connection is, but I think it might help me find him. Precious few people seem interested in helping me, including some of those who should be most concerned. Since I don't know what I'm looking for, it would probably be best for you to just tell me all you know, and even suspect, about her death that night."

A woman walked by with a dainty dog on a purple ribbon leash. "Okay," Doucette said. He waited until she was out of earshot, then began.

"I don't remember whether it was March or April, but it was cold and rainy. You know much about small-town newspapers?"

"No."

"Well, a reporter isn't paid a lot, and the newsroom isn't open after maybe three P.M., so you get most of your tips from the police radio. One advantage is that by definition, you're close to the action in your town, and the Boston papers and stations don't beat you to the scene.

"Well, it must have been about one in the morning, maybe one-thirty. I couldn't sleep that night, so I was dressed, but in bed, reading a novel. I was still living with my parents. I heard his . . . an officer named Gerald Blakey's voice came over the scanner on my bureau."

"I've met him."

Doucette visibly shivered, then continued. "Gerry was calling in to the dispatcher, saying a Mercedes had gone off the Swan Street bridge and was in the water."

"Did Blakey say he saw the car go into the water?"

Doucette finally looked at me as brightly as he had after the call to Mo. "No, which made me wonder how he could know it was a Mercedes. But I'll get to that."

"Sorry," I said. "Go on."

"When I heard Gerry's call, I pulled on a slicker and some boots and drove out there. It was a terrible night for driving. Still, the police station is in Meade Center and my parents live just off Swan, so I had a mile or so lead on the rest of the cops. I got to the bridge first. That is, Gerry was the only one there when I arrived.

"It was raining so hard as I pulled up that I'm not sure he heard me coming. When I slammed the car door, he turned around. He was down at the foot of the bridge, near the water. Have you seen the bridge?"

"Not yet," I said.

"Well, it's on Swan Street, the part of Swan Street as you drive toward the Bonham line. It's maybe half a mile, I don't know, before the Bonham line. Anyway, I pulled in at an angle alongside his cruiser on the Meade side of the bridge.

"When he saw it was me, he came scrambling up the bank, which was quite a sight, with him being so big and the bank so slippery. He was cursing at me when he got to the top. That surprised me, because I hadn't done anything.

"Before he could say anything specific, another cruiser pulled up, lights flashing but no siren, and Chief Smollett in his own car behind it. I remember there were two cops in the cruiser, one with a rope who ran up to Gerry and one who opened the trunk and started pulling scuba equipment out. Smollett came up to me and asked me what the hell I was doing there. Before I could tell him, the cop who'd been with Gerry rushed back and said, 'Chief, Blakey says its Mrs. Kinnington. It's the judge's wife.'

"Smollett broke away and went after Blakey, who now had the rope, down the bank. The other cop ran back to the cruiser to help with the scuba gear. I heard an ambulance siren. It looked pretty crowded down on the bank, so I ran out onto the bridge.

"Some of the railing was broken away, and you could just see the left front side of the car, from about the middle of the driver's window up, and the front of the hood pointing at an angle away from the bridge."

"How far from the bridge?"

"Maybe twenty, twenty-five feet. There's a big rock at that point, and the car was sort of slanting up on it, like the car had tried to drive over the rock and got stuck partway up. Then I—"

"Just a second," I said. "From where you were on the bridge, could you tell it was a Mercedes?"

"No, well, maybe from the hood ornament, but it was raining and blowing so hard, I couldn't make it out."

"Could Blakey have from his angle?"

"No. I looked as closely as I could. That rain was really coming down, and anyway, Gerry, on the bank, was off to the side. In terms of perspective and line of sight, he was directly behind the trunk."

"In those days, cars had license plates on both front and rear. Could Blakey have seen a plate from where he was?"

"No. Nor could I. Both were below water. You couldn't even tell what color the car was, the rain was blowing so hard."

"Go on."

"Let's see. I tried to take a few pictures with my 35 millimeter, but the conditions were pretty hopeless and none of them came out. I was just putting my camera away when the ambulance pulled up. Right about then, the cop with the scuba gear got into the water, and he swam out with a rope around his waist."

"Did he seem to have much trouble with the current?"

"No. But he was swimming hard and I guess he was a pretty strong swimmer, being a diver and all. When he got to the car, he grabbed hold of the door on the driver's side. He yanked on it a few times before it opened."

"Wait a minute. The driver's door was closed?"

"Well, it was hard to tell from where I was. I mean, you really couldn't *see* whether it was closed, but he did seem to be trying to pull it open and was having a hard time. And, like you asked me, it didn't seem like much current. Still, I suppose the door was pushing a lot of water in front of it."

"Go on."

"After he got the door open, he swung his head and shoulders inside, then he turned to the chief and the others on shore. He took his mouthpiece out and yelled, "No body. Nobody inside." The chief waved his hand in a circle over his head, and the diver replaced the mouthpiece and went under. Even with the rain, you could follow his progress by watching the rope. After he zigzagged back and forth on the bridge side of the car a few times, he circled around the car, kind of jump-roping his line over the top of the car. He finally came up, shaking his head, and the chief waved him in to shore. He swam ashore, and then—"

"Any trouble with the current this time?"

"No." Doucette stopped for a moment. "No. In fact, this time he was swimming pretty slowly." Doucette blushed a little. "I remember thinking, 'No rush on the way in. Nobody to save.'"

"What happened then?"

"When he got to shore, Smollett seemed to ask him a few questions, then motioned everybody back up the bank. I trotted back to the cars. Gerry was the first one back. He waved off the ambulance guys, who waited for the chief to tell them to pack it in. I went up to Gerry as he reached his cruiser, and asked him what happened.

"He said 'The judge's wife. Mrs. Kinnington. Her car went off the bridge.'

"I said to him, 'Did you see it happen?'

"He said, 'No. I was driving across the bridge, I saw the railing was broken, and then I saw the car in the water. So I backed up and went down the bank. I couldn't see anybody, so I came back up just as you pulled up.'"

"Did you ask Blakey about his identification of the car?"

"Yes," Doucette grinned. "I asked him how he could tell it was her car, since it was already covered with water. He turned around, looked at the car, turned back, and grabbed my slicker like this"—Doucette clutched and twisted his shirt front—"and slammed me into the side of the cruiser. 'Don't you ever say a fuckin' word about this,' he said to me. 'Or print it. Or you're dead.'" Doucette grew still. "He really meant it."

"Go on."

"Smollett came up and told Gerry to get to the

other side of the bridge—another car had stopped—
to make sure there wasn't another accident. Gerry
said to me, 'Remember,' and sort of sloshed off. Smollett gave me his usual disgusted look, but he walked
back to the other cruiser, where the diver was putting
his equipment back in the trunk.

"I got into my car and drove home. Gerry's threat
had really shaken me. I was just pulling out my house
key when I heard a honk behind me. I turned, and it
was Gerry in the cruiser. He rolled down the window
and said, 'Remember,' again. Just the one word. Then
he drove off. I went in and didn't fall asleep till nine
or ten in the morning. I never wrote the story. I never
really saw Gerry again. I moved to Boston a little
while after that." Doucette paused. "I think that's
about it."

"Ever talk with anyone else about what you saw
and Blakey said?"

"No way. Oh, my parents knew the Kinnington incident was what pushed me to move out. It hit Mom
hard." Doucette cleared his throat and voice. "You've
met Gerry. He and I are the same age. We went to
high school together. He was always so big. He was
never good at athletics, not well-coordinated enough,
I guess. Just big. And aware, painfully aware, of his
hair. He started to lose it when he was a sophomore,
and it was pretty well gone by senior year. Anyway,
one day, our senior year, he and I were walking home
from school, and we started talking, and well, we
went into a bunch of woods and gave each other sex.
He was real nervous, I think it was his first time ever,
and I wasn't very experienced either. Anyway, we left
the woods separately.

"The next day, I was walking to school, and a lot of

guys suspected—funny, I still think of it that way, it's certainly the right word for back then—'suspected' —I was gay. One of them was jibing me that morning. He was a lot bigger than I was, but a lot smaller than Gerry. So, I went up to Gerry between classes and asked him if he'd tell the other guy to lay off me. Well, Gerry grabbed me by the collar and slammed me against the lockers, my books flying all over the place. He hissed at me, 'I don't protect faggots. Now stay away from me.' A bunch of other guys and girls turned around to stare, and Gerry huffed off. I was so embarrassed. It was so bad that the other kids didn't even make fun. I gathered up my books, got to the boys' room, and threw up. Then I cried.

"A few weeks later, I was walking home from school alone. I heard somebody running behind me. I turned, and it was Gerry. He apologized for embarrassing me, and then he asked me to go into the woods again. We did, but this time because I was scared of him. When we were finished, he said, 'You know, if you ever tell anyone about this, I'll kill you. Remember.' He used the same word he used that later time—remember— like maybe his parents used it on him when he was young and he thought it had some magic to it. 'Remember.' "

I thought back to Blakey saying that to me as I left the judge's chambers, but decided it wouldn't help Doucette any. "Did you ever learn anything more about Diane Kinnington's death?"

Doucette shook his head. "No. I mean, I read the newspaper account in the *Banner*, which was just a neutral rehash of a police report. I also read the *Globe* article, which wasn't much more elaborate. And I did know about Mrs. Kinnington's, ah, social life. But

Gerry's threats pretty much blanked me out on her death. In fact, I probably haven't spent as much time on it in the last four years total as I have with you on this bench."

I stretched my legs and stood up. "You've been a big help." He stood and we shook hands. "And no one will ever know I spoke with you."

"One last thing," he said as we walked from the park. "As you know, I guess, Mrs. Kinnington's body was never found. After talking to you today, giving you answers and listening to them myself, I'm pretty sure of something. I think you already figured it, but you weren't there that night and I was."

We'd come to our parting spot, me for my car and him for his office. He stuck his hands in his pockets and looked me straight in the eye. "She wasn't in that car when it went off the bridge. And Gerry Blakey knew it."

He turned and trotted in the heat back toward his office.

Sixteenth

I drove back to the apartment house and double-parked out front. I took the steps two at a time, and just caught the tail end of a dial tone noise as I opened my apartment door. Someone's time for a message had just run out. I waited until I heard the machine turn off with a click, then rewound the tape to playback. There were two messages. The first was from Val:

"John, I've arranged to have us meet Kim at two o'clock at the Sturdevants'. You'll never find it without me, and anyway I don't think Mrs. Sturdevant would talk to you without me there. I don't know how much time I have left—I hate these machines—so pick me up at one-thirty here. I mean here at my house. Remember, 17 Ford . . ."

One admirable thing about the tape. It cuts everyone off equally. The second message, after two hang-ups, was too concise to be affected by the machine's tolerance for talking.

"I regret to report there has been no progress at this end, Mr. Pembroke. You need not contact me."

I thought of Nancy DeMarco and wished that *someone* would make some progress toward finding Stephen.

Apparently, however, I thought and wished too long. By the time I got back downstairs, an orange parking violation card fluttered between my windshield and wiper. I put it in my pocket, stopped at a steak house on the way to Meade, and picked Valerie up at 1:35.

The Sturdevants lived on Fife Street, a string of large, split-level homes about half a mile long on one side of the road. On the other side of the road was apparently untouched forest land. Val said that it was "conservation land," which sounds ecologically advanced but which really means that the town fathers and mothers had voted to buy up vacant land to ensure it would not be developed into new homes or businesses. It also meant that the Sturdevants and other home owners could enjoy in perpetuity gas-fired barbecues and sun decks in their back yards and views of the forest primeval from their front yards.

We stopped the car at 9 Fife, distinguishable from the other splits only by its mailbox label and a bright green upper story over a flat white lower story. I'm sure that the Sturdevants thought the color choice enhanced the "country" look of their neighborhood. Personally, I thought their house looked like a giant 7-Up can somebody had tossed out a car window.

The flagstone path led in a straight line from the edge of the road slightly upgrade to the front door. The neighborhood was *sans* sidewalks, another country affectation.

A woman of perhaps forty answered Valerie's ring. She frowned as she recognized Val. An invisible puff of air-conditioned atmosphere wafted past her to us.

"Hello, Mrs. Sturdevant," began Val. "This is—"

"My husband and I had a talk after I spoke with you, Miss Jacobs," interrupted Mrs. Sturdevant, who was slim and ash-blonde, but with a pinched face and eyes that flickered nervously from Val to me and back again. "We're not at all sure that we should let you talk to Kim about all this. We're afraid it might upset her."

Val looked taken aback, so I slipped into the conversation as gently as I could. "Mrs. Sturdevant, I'm John Cuddy. If I were in your position, I think I'd have the same hesitation. But a boy your daughter's age has disappeared and," I embroidered a bit, "the family is frantic to find him. If we could just come in and talk with you for a few minutes, we'll abide by whatever decision you reach."

The wheels were turning in Mrs. Sturdevant's head. I had the feeling that they turned infrequently, and slowly when they did. "Well," she began and paused. She seemed to have been prepared by Mr. Sturdevant to defend against an assault, but not to decline an invitation to diplomacy.

"Please, Mrs. Sturdevant?" said Val in a soft voice.

Mrs. Sturdevant blinked and relented. "All right, come in."

We followed her into the house. It was dark and quiet inside as well as cool. We turned left and climbed eight low steps to the living room level. A large picture window provided a striking view of the conservation land across the street. In a corner of the room squatted a twenty-five-inch color console television (I believe RCA calls the cabinet "Mediterranean"). The sound was off, but the video displayed some sort of game show. An overweight woman in a red dress was hugging a slim, middle-aged host who smiled enthusiastically. Mrs. Sturdevant took a chair with her back to the TV. Valerie and I took the couch. Although there was a remote control device on the coffee table between us, our hostess made no effort to turn the set off. Perhaps she had become oblivious to it.

"Would you like some coffee and cake?"

Val, remembering my awkwardness at Miss Pitts' house, was about to decline for both of us. I cut her off and said we'd be pleased.

"I'll just be a minute," said Mrs. Sturdevant, who had barely disappeared around a corner before Val turned to me.

"But I thought—"

"You were right," I said, my hand up in a stop sign, "but I wanted a word with you before we tried persuading her." Val nodded and smiled. "Now, as I see it, Mr. S. probably gave her some marching orders and we've altered the conditions. We have to get to her without giving her a need or opportunity to call Mr. S. for further instructions."

"Agreed," said Val, "but in the kitchen she could—"

"Right again. She could call him now. But I'm betting that she has a one-project-at-a-time mindset. Accordingly, I think we're safe for now."

"Safe from what?" spoke a new voice.

Val and I both swiveled around. A much younger version of Mrs. S. stood at the foyer. She had the ash blond hair and slim figure, but her hair was kept in place with a yellow band and her face was open and relaxed. Her eyes only momentarily went toward me before fixing on Valerie.

"Hi, Ms. Jacobs. Safe from what?"

"Hi, Kim," covered Val. "We're talking about Stephen."

At the mention of his name, Kim started running up the stairs toward us and talking at the same time. "Have you heard from him? How is he? Where is he?"

She reached us at the couch just as Mrs. Sturdevant came bustling into the living room, carrying one full coffee cup and one empty one.

"I thought I heard your voice, Kim. We haven't reached a decision yet," she said, parroting my earlier phrase. "Please go to your room." Mom's eyes were nervous still.

"I want to find out about Stephen," said Kim, her eyes steady.

I decided that Mrs. S. probably hadn't won many of these contests recently. "Mrs. Sturdevant." I got up and walked over to her. Val joined us. I lowered my voice with my back toward Kim. "The main concern here is not to upset Kim, right?"

Mrs. Sturdevant looked confused, but she nodded hesitantly.

"Well," I said, "it seems pretty clear that Kim is going to insist on finding out what I can tell her about Stephen." I paused just a beat. "She doesn't strike me as a girl who's going to take no for an answer."

Mrs. Sturdevant nodded again. The cups were rattling against their saucers in her slightly trembling hands. "She is a very determined girl sometimes."

I gave Val a gentle nudge, a signal we'd worked out on the drive over.

"Mrs. Sturdevant, why don't you and I go into the kitchen. I guarantee that Mr. Cuddy will be very careful with Kim and not do anything you'd disapprove of."

"Well . . . " said Mrs. Sturdevant.

"Mom," said Kim clearly and stubbornly. "I'm going to find out about Stephen."

"Well," said Mrs. Sturdevant, thus prodded. "If you think it's best . . . "

"I know it is," said Val, relieving the woman of the formerly full, now slightly spilled, cup and guiding her toward the kitchen.

Kim and I were alone. She was wearing running shorts and a halter top, small breasts just pushing out against the fabric. Her feet were bare, her toenails painted the bright pink of her lipstick. I had the feeling that the lipstick went on after Daddy left in the morning and came off before Daddy got home at night. She had a Sony Walkman strapped around her waist, the light earphone attachment resting on her shoulders like a bizarre necklace.

"It's your house," I said, "but why don't we sit down?"

She gave a little frown, then sat in her mother's chair. I don't think Kim noticed that the TV was on either, but the woman in the red dress must have done well again, because she was again hanging on the host, who was still smiling, but only sportingly now.

"Who are you?" Kim asked warily.

"My name is John Cuddy," I said, handing her a card and even flashing her my identification. I thought it might impress her, but she barely glanced at it. "I'm a private detective. I've been hired to try to find Stephen. I'm hoping that you can help me."

She shook her head. "I don't know where he is. I thought you'd be able to tell me how he is."

We looked at each other for a moment. I had the feeling that Kim's wheels turned faster and a lot more frequently than her mother's.

I sighed in what I hoped was a reassuring way.

"Kim, I was hired by Stephen's grandmother, not his father. His father, for reasons I can't imagine, doesn't seem much interested in finding Stephen. Valerie—Ms. Jacobs—and I have been chasing down every lead we can find. She told me you and Stephen were good friends, that maybe you could help."

Kim settled back into the chair. Her left hand began to fiddle with the earphones around her neck. "Ms. Jacobs said Stephen and I were good friends?" she asked.

I sensed an opening. "Actually, I asked her who was closest to Stephen in the class, and she said you were."

Kim flushed a little, partly from pride, partly from embarrassment. Mostly from pride, though.

"Stephen's a hard person to get close to," she said. "He and I went to different schools till last year, and last year's homeroom was alphabetical. You know, they'd assign us to rooms based on our last names. Then somebody got the idea that alphabetical assignment was 'stultifying.' That's the word the principal used this year, 'stultifying.' So they just assigned us randomly." She smiled. "So this was the first year I had a lot of classes with Stephen."

I leaned back in the couch. "I've seen photographs of Stephen, but I've never met him. What's he like?"

She eyed me for a moment and decided I was sincere. "He's the smartest guy I've ever met. There are a lot of kids at our school who are great test-takers, even without studying or anything, you know. But Stephen is really different. He's smart past everybody, even the teachers, way past." She gave me a smug smile. "He's a genius. He could be anything. Anything he wants."

"What *does* Stephen want?" I asked.

She frowned, but not at me. "I don't know," she said quietly, looking down at her lap.

Dead end. Back up and try another street.

"When did you last see Stephen before he disappeared?"

"It must have been the day he left. We were in school together. We had a morning class, one of those nothing classes you have when exams are over. Then we had lunch." She smiled again. "We ate lunch together, at one of the picnic tables outside school."

"Did he say anything that indicated why he was leaving or where he was going?"

She frowned again, this time at me. "No," she said, a little too certainly.

I sighed and spread my hands in front of me. "Look,

109

Kim, I will not reveal to anyone anything you tell me."

She eyed me cautiously. "Like lawyers and clients?"

I shook my head. "I won't bullshit you, Kim. There is no detective-confidential source privilege in Massachusetts. But that just means that I might go to jail for keeping quiet about what you tell me. It doesn't mean I won't keep my word. I will." I leaned forward again. "I think Stephen's in trouble because someone is after him. I don't know why someone's after him, and I'm not sure you do. I *am* sure that if I don't get more information about Stephen, I'm never going to find him."

She dropped the frown and resumed her fiddling with the earphones. "Maybe he doesn't want to be found."

I resisted the temptation to ask her why she might think that. "Kim, please trust me."

She shook her head. "Stephen once told me not to trust anyone. He said he didn't trust anyone."

"He trusted you," I said, quietly.

She smiled sadly. "No, not much." She wiped at her eye, then said, "Look, mister, I don't know where Stephen is. I don't even know why he left. I was hoping you could tell me he was okay. If you can't, you can't. If I can't, I can't. Okay?"

This time I shook my head more emphatically. "No. Not okay. I care about Stephen. I care because he's had a tough life of it so far, and it's my job to find him. But you care *for* him, and despite what you've said so far, I think he did trust you with something, with some information. There is no way I can make you trust me, but I don't see how you can think Stephen is better off out there than back here with us protecting him."

She glared at me. "Us! Us protecting him? It's his father who's after him. The judge and Blakey. How can you protect Stephen from them?"

"I don't know," I said, "but maybe the reason Stephen ran would give me leverage enough to do that."

" 'Leverage,' " she snorted sarcastically. "That's what my father uses to close computer sales. That's how you're going to stop the judge?"

"Kim, I don't know what your image of the judge and his power is, but nobody is all-powerful. There are things, facts or evidence, that can scare the judge, same as you or me. If Stephen knows or found out something, and that knowledge or fact was important enough to make him run, it may be important enough to bring him back and protect him from the judge." I paused. "What do you say?"

The glare slid away, and she chewed her lower lip. "I'm just so scared for him," she said, the tears welling up.

I dug out a handkerchief and she cried quietly into it for about ten seconds. Then she wiped her eyes and nose. "What do you want to know?" She was flushed and red-eyed, but cooperative.

"What did you and Stephen talk about at lunch that day?"

She sniffed and began. "The same thing we always talked about. His quest."

"His quest? You mean, like a search or a mission?"

"Yes. Stephen and I got to be, like Ms. Jacobs said, close. I kind of watched him last year and the beginning of this year. He's real intelligent-looking and, well, anyway, I saw that he didn't seem to have any friends. I mean, he would talk to the other kids, but just kind of politely, like he was talking to a teacher or somebody's father and he didn't want any trouble. I think he just wasn't much interested in what the kids were doing and talking about. Like, whenever he talked with me, it was like we were on a different level from the rest of the kids."

"You mentioned his quest."

"Yes, I'm coming to that. One day I just sort of decided to try talking—really talking—to him. That was this year, maybe October or November." She paused. "It was November, because the decorations were up. You know, the stupid stuff like cardboard turkeys and pilgrims?"

"I know."

"Well, we just started talking, and it was amazing, you know, the way he could explain things and understand the things I would say. It was like . . . it was like he was the best teacher I ever had, but he was my own age—actually a year older because he . . . lost a year. He understood me, but he acted older, so I could . . . I could . . . "

"Respect him?" I said tactfully.

She sniffed again. "Yeah, respect him. Anyway, it was maybe two months ago that he told me about his mother, and how he'd gotten sick and was in the hospital."

"Did he tell you what kind of illness he had?"

She fixed me with her still-reddish eyes. "Yeah, mental illness. He was in a crazy house, out in the mountains somewhere. His father did it."

I tensed. "Did what?"

"Huh?"

"You said, 'his father did it.' What did his father do?"

"Oh, his father put him in the crazy house. His grandmother didn't want him to stay there, though, but he still had to stay a long time, like maybe a year. When he got out, he came home. That's when he began his quest."

I held onto my patience. "What was Stephen's quest?"

Kim became very still. She looked down. "You have to promise never to tell anyone."

I promised.

"You can't even ever tell Stephen I told you. I'm the only one who knows, so you can't even let him know you know or he'd know it was me."

"I promise," I repeated.

She twisted the earphones off her neck and played with them in her lap. I involuntarily noticed that the woman in the red dress must have won again. This time she was literally smothering the host, who was no longer smiling, sportingly or otherwise. Kim's first words snapped me back.

"His mother was killed. Murdered. His quest was to get evidence. To prove his father did it." She shivered.

I gave her a moment, then: "Kim, what kind of evidence?"

She began gnawing on her lower lip again. "A gun."

"A gun?"

"Yes," she said.

"Stephen's mother supposedly died in a car accident. Stephen believed his mother was shot?"

Kim, crying again, now nodded vigorously. I heard soft footsteps, Valerie's, I thought, approach and recede. I could just hear Val's voice from the kitchen.

She said, "They're doing fine, Mrs. Sturdevant."

I wasn't sure how much more Kim had left.

"Why did he think that, Kim? Why did he think his mother was shot?"

"Because," she said, too loudly, nearly a wail. She dropped her voice. "Because he was there."

She fell silent. Me too. Then, "Kim, at that last lunch, did Stephen say anything about being in danger, or . . ."

She blew her nose and fixed me again. "You don't understand," she said. "He'd found it. That was what he told me at lunch. The quest was over. He'd found the gun."

"He'd found it?"

"Yes. The night before. Every night he'd wait until everyone was asleep. Then he'd search a different place. He thought his father might suspect he was on the quest, so sometimes Stephen would double back and re-check some of the old places. But he finally found it."

"Did he say what he was going to do with it?"

"No." She managed a half-smile. "No. He had been on the quest for so long, years, that I don't think he really had figured out what he was going to do. I mean exactly what he was going to do. When he found it." She wiped her eyes again.

"Kim, I think Stephen left on his own. And from what you've told me, I'm sure it was because of finding the gun. Is there anything else you can tell me about Stephen, like where he might go?"

She shook her head. "He never—"

She stopped and froze as the big front door clicked and then banged open. "Sal, Kim. I'm home. Hey, Sal, I may be early but—"

I swiveled around and rose. A bearish, balding guy

of forty-five or so came tromping up the stairs to the living room. I caught Kim rubbing furiously on her lips with my handkerchief as he saw us and exploded.

"Who are you? Kim! What the hell is that stuff doing on your—You're crying!"

By this time a terrified Mrs. Sturdevant, with Val in her wake, burst into the room.

"Hal, oh Hal," she cried, "they said it would be all right."

I remember nearly laughing. Val, Sal, and now Hal. But there was nothing humorous about Hal just then.

"You're the guy we told to stay away, aren't you?" Hal's briefcase, newspaper, and a supermarket bag hit the carpet. A widening pool of milk gurgled out of an unseen carton.

"Mr. Sturdevant, I'm investigating . . ."

He swung a rounding left as Sal screamed his name and Val yelled mine. I ducked under it and just pushed him, but hard, with my open hands as his shoulder went over my head. It knocked him off balance, and his momentum was broken by banging into the wall.

I spoke as quickly as I could. "This is your home, Mr. Sturdevant. I have no desire or reason to hurt you. I will leave immediately if you tell me to."

Sturdevant came off the wall and hesitated. Sally grabbed his arm. "Please Hal, just tell him to go."

Hal, his honor saved by her entreaty, glared at me. I noticed for the first time that Kim was gone. I had a vague recollection of a slamming door in there somewhere.

"Get out! Get out of my house and don't ever come back!"

I nodded and backed toward the stairs. I motioned to Val to precede me down, which she did. The Sturdevants, Hal leading and Sal in tow, followed us down, maintaining a three-step interval.

"Get out. Get out. Get out!" The last shout cracked his voice a bit.

We were outside. Sturdevant slammed the door behind us. We had reached our car when I heard a window open. I turned around in time to see Kim's head and forearms pop out an upper story window.

"Tell Stephen," she sobbed, "tell him that I love him. Tell him . . . " at which point a pair of fatherly hands pinned her elbows, yanked her from the opening, and slammed the window as well.

A tearful Val spoke as I opened the car door for her. "Somebody else does care for Stephen."

"Yeah," I said, "for all the good it's done him so far."

Seventeenth

I dropped Val off at her place. She apologized for having to rush off to meet her friend, and I assured her that I'd see her for dinner the next night. As I backed out of her driveway, I checked my watch. Three-thirty. A little early for court to be over, I hoped.

I drove down several now-familiar Meade byways until I reached the Kinnington driveway. I swung into the drive and up, parking it in a position that would let me leave quickly, and knocked at the door. Mrs. Page opened it a crack, into which I introduced my foot. We both spoke at the same time.

"Mrs. Kinnington?"

"Go away!"

The door jarred against my foot.

"You're crazy to come here."

"I have to see her, Mrs. Page."

The pressure relaxed.

"Upstairs," she sighed. "Same room."

At the room, I knocked and entered.

This time I had to pull the strong chair over myself. Otherwise, the scene was unchanged.

"You have word of Stephen?" she asked.

"Yes and no. I've received some words that encourage me and other words that I should have heard first from my client. That's you."

"Mr. Cuddy, I am not used to being addressed—"

"And I am not used to playing Blind Bozo bumbling in the dark. At least not in unnecessary darkness. Why didn't you tell me what Miss Pitts saw?"

Her eyes dropped to examine her teacup.

"It is not the type of thing one discusses."

"Maybe not at the D.A.R., Mrs. Kinnington, but to the detective who's looking—"

"That's quite enough!" she snapped, the teacup rattling against its saucer. "You damn, self-righteous bastard! You're my employ*ee*, not my employ*er*. You may be a professional, but you're *my* professional. You'll do what you're told and be satisfied with what you're told or you can resign."

I stood up. "My resignation will be on your desk in the morning, ma'am," I said. I dropped her original print of Stephen's photo on the table and turned to leave.

"Mr. Cuddy," she said, her voice wavering, "are you close to him?"

"Mrs. Kinnington," I said over my shoulder, "I'm closer than I was the last time we had this argument."

Her voice steadied. "Please sit down again."

The air seemed a bit freer. I sat. "Why didn't you tell me about Stephen and Blakey?"

She re-seated her teacup in the saucer. "It's so troubling to think that there could be any relationship between them that . . . Stephen has always been so indifferent to the judge. I just assumed that the . . . edge between Stephen and Blakey was a function of Blakey's being my son's . . . oh, henchman."

"Henchman?"

"Well, that's just how Blakey has always struck me. As a doer of evil things. I even forbade the judge to allow Blakey to come into the same room with me. Consequently, when Miss Pitts called me, I realized I was in no position to be able to say what there was between Stephen and Blakey."

"Mrs. Kinnington, I have to assume that Stephen left voluntarily." I remembered my promise to Kim Sturdevant. "But I still need to know what reason he might have had for leaving."

She clasped her hands in her lap and tried to relax. "Mr. Cuddy, I do not know why Stephen would have gone. He did not get along with his father, but I know of no recent incident that could have triggered Stephen's disappearance."

"Speaking of triggered," I asked, bending my promise to Kim a bit, "did Stephen have a gun?"

Her throat worked once before the sound came out. "A gun?"

"Yes."

"Why do you want to know about guns?"

"Please, Mrs. Kinnington."

She considered. "My son, that is, Stephen's Uncle Telford, left him a pistol in his, ah, will. Some sort of fancy target pistol. To start him properly. Stephen, almost before he could write, would shoot at targets on the grounds with Beeman, who was the houseman then. But I haven't seen the gun, or Stephen with a weapon of any kind, in years."

"Well, he has one now," I said as I rose.

"How do you know that?"

I ignored her question, substituting one of my own. "By the way, was a gun all that Stephen and Telford shared?"

She looked at me suspiciously. "Now what do you mean by that?"

"I have reason to believe that Telford was institutionalized, or nearly so, while he was in the service. Stephen was institutionalized after his mother's death. Could it be that mental illness runs in your family, Mrs. Kinnington?"

"That's preposterous, and I'll not have you spreading a story like that."

"I'm not," I said with my hand on the doorknob, "but Stephen and his gun might be."

"Mr. Cuddy, do you know where Stephen is or not?"

"No, I don't. But in view of Blakey's involvement and temperament, I'd be afraid to tell you if I did."

As I pulled out of the Kinnington driveway, my mind was working on the most direct route to the Mass Pike. As I skirted Meade Center, I went past a large public building on my right. There was a sign just beneath the flagpole. I hit my brakes and eased to the curb. From what Val and Mrs. Kinnington had told me of Stephen's reading habits, he must have out-distanced the contents of his school's library years ago. It was a longshot, but I was pretty much down to longshots right then.

The public library was itself a restored quasi-mansion, red brick with four white columns. There was a meticulous expanse of lawn and a semicircular parking lot. Inside, the librarian was a pleasant change of pace from most Meade residents I'd met. She was polite.

I identified myself and explained that Ms. DeMarco and I were looking into Stephen's disappearance. Since I was out here speaking with Mrs. Kinnington anyway, I thought I'd stop by and check Stephen's library borrowings. I wasn't sure if Ms. DeMarco had done so yet.

Her middle-age face grew concerned. "You know, I wondered whether someone was still looking into that. Such a poor, unfortunate family. First Telford, then Diane—they were the judge's brother and wife, you know—and now Stephen. The whole town is whispering about it, but nobody really knows anything yet. You make yourself comfortable and I'll be right back." She walked back into an inner office behind the counter. She came back with a tray of perhaps a hundred old-style computer cards and set it on the counter.

"By the way," she said extending her hand, "I'm Madeline Moore." I shook her hand and she gave it a little extra squeeze *à la* Valerie—but in a friendly rather than sensual way.

"Pleased to meet you, Ms. Moore."

She looked down and flipped through a few cards. "You know, I nearly cursed the idea of a computer system for borrowers. Imagine, a computer in Meade! but I must say it *is* more efficient once you get the hang of it. Here."

She slid the tray gently toward me. "Stephen read all these books?" I asked.

"Oh, my, he's read many more than these. These are just the ones he took out since January. He'd also spend every afternoon after school here in the reading room, literally devouring the books and magazines. I never saw the like of him, poor boy."

I began to flip through the cards the way she had. Almost all were novels or historical works. Two I came upon dealt with camping. I was about to ask her if I could see those when a photocopier began hiccupping behind me. It was one of those open-topped machines for use with books. I hadn't noticed it when I came in.

"Did you see Stephen photocopying any maps recently?" I asked.

"Maps? No-o-o, but now that you mention it, I did see him photocopying something that was in an issue of *New England Outdoors*. In fact, it wasn't too long before he disappeared. I never would have thought about it if you hadn't asked me. You see, many of the ah . . . young boys try to copy certain, well, advertisements for, ah, women's clothes, and I never thought Stephen was that type, but when I came close to him as he was copying something, he became secretive, so I wondered if I was wrong about him. But I watched him put the magazine back, and I checked on it and was relieved. I just never thought about it after that."

"Do you remember what issue it was?"

"I think so," she said as she came out from behind the desk and walked over to some periodical racks. "It was," she said, thumbing through the magazines, "this one."

Just as she handed it to me, her phone began ringing. She left me to answer it and I sat down in a stuffed leather chair.

I opened to the table of contents. Five lead articles, six departments on camping subspecialities. I skimmed the articles. The third one was about the great number of abandoned, tower-style ranger stations and the dangers in using them as shelters. The article mentioned that there were thirty-seven such stations north of New Jersey and it named several. Four were spread widely over the Berkshire Mountains of western Massachusetts. One page of the article was a map showing the stations. I looked up. The copying machine took dimes.

As I left the machine, I waved to my helpful friend, who gave me a can't-you-stay-till-I-get-off-the-phone? look. I couldn't.

As soon as I left the library, I began looking for a pay telephone. I found one outside a superette market on Meade's main drag and dialed Valerie's number. No answer, indicating that she had left to meet her friend in Boston. I hung up and tried the Kinningtons. The judge answered. I hung up and drummed my fingers on the little metal counter that's too narrow to write on and too slanted to rest coins on. I dialed directory assistance and got the Sturdevants' number. I called hoping for Kim and raised old Hal instead. I hung up on him, too.

I jackknifed open the telephone booth door and went back to my car. I took out the *New England Outdoors* page I'd photocopied and studied the small-scale map on it. I had a rough idea where the Willow Wood sanatorium was, but none of the ranger stations were very close to it. The two farthest stations were at least sixty-five miles away from each other and probably not easily accessible by car. Which meant a day or two of scouting them out, assuming Stephen would be in the last one I'd check. Assuming that he was in any of the stations. Assuming that this was the article he had copied. Assuming that Ms. Moore was right about which issue he'd had.

The alternative was to try to find out if there was any faster way to trace him to one of the stations. Valerie still seemed the best bet for that, and I could call her later tonight or earlier tomorrow than I could either Mrs. Kinnington or Kim. I folded up the map and drove impatiently homeward against the rush-hour flow.

Eighteenth

I picked up a bucket of chicken at the Kentucky Fried on Brighton Avenue in Allston, once again bemoaning the passing of the franchise that had been diagonally across from my apartment on Charles Street. I wrestled the rental into a parallel parking space with six inches to spare front and back.

The red light on my telephone tape machine was lit, but I decided it could wait until after dinner. I washed the chicken down with two Molson Golden Ales and settled into an easy chair with one of Robert B. Parker's Spenser novels. I had read four pages when a telephone in the novel began ringing. Memory jogged, I put the book down, walked to my telephone machine, and replayed the short message. I replayed it several times. The muffled voice on the other end said only the same one word each time:

"Remember."

The chicken parts in my stomach made an effort to reassemble themselves. I had another Molson's to calm them down.

I tried Val's number every half hour up to and including 11:30. I know, because I could recall seeing Johnny Carson's monologue but drew a blank on his guests. I stretched stiffly in the easy chair. The clock on the mantel said 4:15. I went to bed, resetting my clock radio for 6:15. I awakened to Deep Purple's classic "Smoke on the Water" on WCOZ (whose motto is "Kick-ass rock and roll"). I splashed some water in my face and called Valerie.

It rang four times before I got a sleepy "Hullo."

"Val, it's John Cuddy."

"Oh, hi, John. I must have over—hey, it's only six-thirty!"

"Yeah, I'm sorry, but I might be on to something."

"Oh, really?" she said, in my mind's eye sitting up in bed and pushing her hair back. "What is it?"

"Remember when we were on the beach, with those guys playing football?"

"Hmph. I'll never forget it."

"I asked you about what transportation Stephen might use, and you said you couldn't think of any."

"Right."

"How about the Berkshires?"

"The Berkshires? The mountains or the region in general?"

"Either. Whatever. Did Stephen ever talk with you about the Berkshires?"

She paused. "No, not that I can think of. Why the Berkshires?"

"Well, a couple of things. Someone saw him looking at a magazine with an article on them. He also spent time in a mental institution out there, so he might know a little more about that area and therefore head that way."

"Stephen was so interested in so many things, but I can't think of anything—Wait a minute! He did do a social studies paper once about how . . . oh, what was it? Meat, that's right, meat! He had written it for another teacher, but was proud of it so he wanted me to see it. It involved how meat went from somewhere in Boston all over the state by truck. I'm pretty sure part of it dealt with the Berkshires."

"Kind of thin. But I think I know where to start."

"Oh, John, will you still be able to come for dinner tonight?"

"It depends."

"On what?"

I debated a lie. "I'll be there," I said.

"Terrific. Seven o'clock?"

"You bet."

She giggled. "See you then."

"Bye-bye."

I hung up and checked the clock. This would be the busy time down at the meat exchange and I wanted to get there when the boys had a little time to talk, so I did a long-for-me six miles to run off the chicken and the Molsons, trying not to think about the voice on the tape, which I knew but could never prove was Blakey's. I had breakfast and decided on a T-shirt and Levis for the trip to the market.

The meat exchange is nestled in a noisy bunch of hangarlike buildings just off the Southeast Expressway on the southern outskirts of Boston. It was nearly 10:00 by my watch, which meant that the man I wanted to see had been on the job for five hours already. I parked the rental and walked into the biggest of the structures. I was struck by the cool, nearly overpowering atmosphere of fresh but dead animal meat. I turned two interior corners before I saw Al raising his cleaver.

Al Bufone is five-five in height and three-five in width. When he picks up a meat cleaver, it looks like an old-fashioned straight razor in comparison to his hands. He sports three navy tattoos from the South Pacific on his right arm and a few wispy black hairs in a clump at the top of his forehead. He looked up and saw me.

"John, boy, whaddaya say?"

"Not much, Al. Yourself?"

"No complaints." He whacked twice with the cleaver. "Rose and me hit the doggies Monday. Missed the double by a nose, but we did awright otherwise. Hey," he said, hefting a veal leg, "can you use some?"

"No, thanks, Al. Could use some information, though."

Al set down the veal leg and wiped his hand on his apron as he looked around carefully.

"B and E or hijack?" he asked softly.

"Neither," I replied, reflexively looking around too. Some people don't like other people talking to insurance investigators about certain transactions. "I'm looking for a fourteen-year-old boy."

Al laughed. "I heard you went out on your own. Where's the kid from?"

"Meade."

Al laughed harder.

"Oh, yeah, sure John-boy. He's in the fuckin' back room sweepin' scraps. This was the first place his guidance counselor *referred* him."

"He's a runaway, Al. I thought he might try to cop a ride from here to the Berkshires on one of the trucks." I showed him Stephen's photo.

"Nah," said Al. "I've never seen him before."

As I drew the photo back, he said, "Wait a minute." He looked at it again. "Y'know, there was a kid here, mebbe two weeks ago. But he looked older than fourteen. He also had blondish hair, y'know. But his eyes looked like that kid's eyes. Sorta deep 'n' sad, y'know."

I felt hope rising.

"Did you talk to him?"

"No. I remember Vinnie sayin' somethin' about the kid writin' an article for his school paper on somethin'."

"Where's Vinnie?"

"I haven't seen him today. But I'm pretty sure Sammy DiLeo talked to the kid too. Sammy just got in from Pittsfield a half hour ago."

Pittsfield, the major city in the Berkshires. "Where can I find Sammy?"

Al gestured toward the loading docks. "He should be checkin' on the load he's takin'. Probably Dock Two."

"Thanks, Al." I started walking.

"Oh, John-boy. Mind Sammy now. He's kind of a weaselly bastard."

"Thanks," I repeated, and kept walking.

Dock Two was off by itself, a large overhead garage door that opened to the sunshine. As I approached it, I could see two men arguing in the open mouth of the back of a refrigerated trailer truck. The air grew warmer and the smell of meat less striking as I moved toward the truck.

"Sammy, you goddamn thief, I'm not fuckin' short and you know it. Every case on that invoice is in this fuckin' truck."

"Look, George, either you reduce the fuckin' bottom line on this invoice or I make you unload this fuckin' truck and recount on your fuckin' time."

George was getting redder and redder, shaking his clipboard like a war shield.

"Every time you do this, Sammy. Every fuckin' time."

"Refigure or unload," said Sammy with a smirk.

George turned and stomped away. "I'm gettin' Al."

"Al can't change the union contract, George," smiled Sammy as George passed me. Sammy reached into his pocket and pulled out his keys as I approached him.

"Shouldn't you wait for Al?" I said.

Sammy gave me the defender-against-invader look. "Who the fuck are you?"

"John Cuddy," I said. "I'm looking for a young boy."

Sammy sneered. "Whasamatter, wife got lockjaw?"

I decided where I was going to hit him, but not when. "I'm a private detective." I showed him Stephen's picture. "His hair would have been blonder," I said.

As Sammy looked at the picture, a faint flush spread up to his neck, then faded. "Nah, never seen him. I gotta go." He half-turned and fumbled with his keys.

"I'm told you and the boy had a talk two weeks ago."

He turned back and tried to stare me down. "Oh, yeah? Who says?"

"A man you'd best not suggest is a liar."

He blinked. "Fuck you. I gotta go."

I caught his arm and spun him into some stacked crates nearby. His momentum led him to sit down awkwardly and heavily on one of them.

"The boy is missing. You're the last one to see him. How does a morals charge strike you?"

"You haven't got shit. Whaddaya mean morals charge? You callin' me a fag?" He flexed for me.

"No, but I'm suggesting the boy might be gay. Where do you suppose that leaves you?"

Sammy thought about that and didn't like his position. "I thought his hair looked a little funny."

"What happened?"

"Look, man, nothin' happened. Just nothin'. He asked me for a lift to the mountains so he could go on some kinda reportin' trip. He had a backpack and everything."

"Where in the mountains?"

"Granville. It's a little town way northwest, maybe four miles off the Pike, Lee exit."

"Where did you drop him off?"

"About a half mile before Granville Center."

"If he was going on a reporting trip, why didn't he ride all the way into town?"

Sammy sneered again. "He didn't fuckin' say."

I leaned over. "Sammy, I think you tried to shake him down."

Sammy swung a left at me as he rose. His left was a little slower than it should have been. I deflected it and him to my left with my left palm and gave him a moderate cupped-hand dig in the back, near his left kidney. He sagged down, doubled over.

"What did you try to charge him for the lift, Sammy?"

"Jesus . . . I think you ruptured . . . somethin'!"

"Sammy, answer my question! How much?"

"Twenny bucks. I saw . . . he had plenty . . . when he paid . . . one of the tolls."

"He paid up, did he?"

"Yeah, yeah."

I lifted his chin up gently. "Sammy, I don't believe you. And I don't think the cops will either."

"Awright, awright. He didn't pay. But I didn't make him. . . . He just hopped out and . . . ran."

"With a pack he outdistanced you? Do you figure your kidney needs a little more massage, Sammy?"

"No, no. He . . . ah, listen, man—you gotta keep this quiet. Around here, I'd be laughed at. I'd be laughed outta' the place." He winced and gritted his teeth. "Jesus, you hurt me."

"Come on, Sammy."

"Okay, okay. He had a piece."

"A piece?"

"A gun, man. A long thing like outta *Star Wars.* He fuckin' went into his pack for the twenny and come out with the piece. I thought the fuckin' little screwy was gonna shoot me. I backed off, and he took off across a field."

I straightened up. "Thanks, Sammy. You've been a swell guy and a great panelist."

As I walked away I heard the telltale click. I wheeled around as Sammy was coming off the crate with a big clasp knife open for business. His face was still contorted in pain, but a vengeful determination shone through.

The booming voice behind me interrupted our little melodrama. "Sammy, you drop the knife or it's the last piece of anything your fingers'll ever go 'round."

I glanced over my shoulder at Al with his cleaver hanging at his side and a somewhat calmer George next to him.

Sammy didn't close the knife, but he visibly stood down. I walked toward Al and thanked him.

"I told ya he was a weaselly bastard," replied Al as I passed on my way out.

Nineteenth

"I'm not sure how far it is to Granville, but I expect it's going to be an overnighter. You know how I hated to travel without you. And I can't very well call you, you know."

The carnations weren't there anymore. The kid in the jeans had probably scoffed them as soon as I'd left the last time. I squatted down and arranged Mrs. Feeney's red roses on the spot where the carnations had been.

"The grandmother hasn't played straight with me, Beth. I think I know where the kid is, or at least where he was headed, because one of the ranger stations is only four miles from Granville. But I have to check out a few things first."

A puff of wind came off the Harbor and ruffled the roses. I foraged a rock to hold them down.

Off to the left, at another grave, I noticed an elderly man. He wore an old gray suit and held a Homburg in his hand. He was motionless, standing to the side of a headstone and staring at it.

I looked down at Beth. Funny, I almost never looked at the stone. Probably because the stone wasn't her, wasn't where she was for me.

"This boy I'm looking for, Stephen, must be some piece of work. His teachers think he's at least exceptional and a doll in his class thinks he's a genius and is crazy about him. His father seems not to care about him, his grandmother seems not to care about much anything else. He's apparently shy around most kids, but he has perseverance enough to search his father's house for a gun for four years, and then balls enough to take off and use the gun to stand off a shake-down artist twice his size."

Something was wrong there. Like always, Beth sensed it before I did. But I couldn't quite put it into a thought, and she couldn't put it into words.

I needed to get something else off me and squared away, anyway. I took a breath and hunched down again.

"I did a necessary thing this afternoon, Beth. I roughed up a cheating, lying trucker. He was the shake-down artist. But I did a stupid thing before that. I spidered a big, bullying college kid into a short fight and humiliation. It wasn't just my overeager sense of righteousness, Beth. I was showing off. Showing off for somebody I was with. Valerie. Sort of the way I showed off for you. But not quite. For you I showed off *for* you. For Valerie, I showed off just to see that I could still show off for somebody. Pretty dumb, not to mention a pretty boring description of being dumb. But then, you always put up with dumb, boring me much better than most."

I laughed for her, then got serious again. "Valerie took offense, but I apologized and it's okay now. Except that she's invited me to dinner, and I'm afraid she's getting the wrong impression, that she thinks that I'm—"

I stopped because Beth and I had come to a decision. It certainly seemed the only fair thing.

I stood up. The mini-yachts of the well-to-do who lived on the renovated waterfront were tacking and running in the harbor below. I looked down at the grave. Mrs. Feeney had done a nice job with the roses.

As I walked out of the cemetery, the elderly man with the Homburg was still standing over the other grave. Still motionless.

Twentieth

I stopped at the apartment. My tape had two hang-ups. I reset the machine and changed my clothes. I figured it would be colder in the Berkshires and I wasn't sure when I would be able to change again. I put on a flannel shirt and a pair of khaki pants. I strapped my Chief's Special to my inside left calf and bloused the pant bottoms into the tops of a pair of L. L. Bean Maine hunting boots. I slung an old Army pack (with a jacket, canteen, and candy bars) over my shoulder.

There was some plain white bond paper on my desk. I took a piece and wrote a short note, marked the envelope "Personal," and put a return address under the name "Pembroke." I mailed it on my way back to the car. Then I headed southwest.

The sun was still high, and children were out sunning and playing ball in seemingly every yard and field I passed. There was a constant gentle breeze of the kind that I remembered kept you from getting thirsty. The flannel shirt was making me thirsty.

I took the exit that would bring me to Bonham Center first. Since Cal was a six-days-a-week cop, I stopped in at police headquarters and was told Chief Maslyk would be back in an hour. I had a late lunch at an uncrowded pub with a jukebox that played country-and-western. I returned to the station, and still had to cool my heels for twenty minutes until Cal Maslyk could see me.

I told him about my planned trip to the Berkshires. He asked me why I was telling him, and I said because I might need someone to come looking for me. He said he had some vacation time coming in September and that if I weren't back by then, he'd swing by Granville to check on me. I thanked him and left.

It was only 4:00 and I couldn't see dropping in on Val that early. I decided to drive over to the Swan Street bridge. Thomas Doucette had already poked a lot of holes for me in Blakey's version of Diane Kinnington's accident, but a law professor of mine always had stressed that we actually should visit the scene of any incident.

I crisscrossed Bonham roads for thirty minutes without hitting Swan Street. I ended back in Bonham Center. Too proud to stop and ask directions, I took a road with a sign that said "Meade Center 3." Just past the center I came upon Swan Street. As I prepared to turn north onto it, a Meade police car drove through the intersection heading south. Officer Dexter was in the passenger's seat. He seemed to recognize me. I waved to him, but he didn't wave back.

I turned onto Swan Street back toward Bonham and drove a little over a mile before seeing the bridge ahead. I was surprised. I had expected the bridge to be around a corner or curve, but it was clearly visible along the straight road for nearly four-tenths of a mile. Diane Kinnington, or anyone else, would have had no corner or curve to negotiate that night.

When I reached the bridge, I slowed and checked my rear-view mirror. There was no traffic behind me. I slowed to a crawl and went across the bridge as Blakey told Doucette he had done that rainy night. As Doucette had described it, there was a rock maybe twenty feet out whose crest was eight inches clear of the water line. There were replacement railings where Diane's car must have gone through, but the car couldn't have been going very fast to land so close to the bridge. I studied the spot where the Mercedes must have rested. When I reached the other end of the bridge, I stopped and got out. Again I looked to where the Mercedes must have been. Then I checked for traffic, backed across the bridge, and angled my car in the way Doucette had placed Blakey's cruiser. I tried to keep my eyes focused on the rock and the placement of the Mercedes as I sidestepped down the embankment. I stood at the river's edge and stared across to the other bank. If Doucette was accurate regarding the Mercedes's reclining angle against the rock in the water and the compass angle to the far shore, there was no way that Blakey could have seen a license plate or even a hood ornament to know it was the Kinnington car out there.

I heard a car crunch to a stop above me. I turned and looked up as a second car pulled alongside the first. Both were Meade police cruisers. Dexter and a big officer I hadn't seen before got out of the first cruiser. Chief Smollett and another big cop got out of the second cruiser. All came to the upper edge of the embankment and stared down at me. I stared back.

Smollett put his fists on his hips and broke the stand-off. He wore a uniform parade hat, but civilian gray shirt and pants. "I thought I told you to get out and stay out of this town."

"Sorry to have to correct you, Chief," I replied as good-naturedly as possible, "but you told me only to *get* out of your *office*. You said nothing about town or about *staying* out, for that matter."

The two big cops turned expectantly to Smollett. Dexter looked down at his shoes. Smollett looked down at me.

"You been bothering our citizens," Smollett continued, not raising his voice. Now everyone was looking down at me again.

"Just which citizen or citizens am I supposed to have bothered?"

Smollett's jaw worked a little before he answered. "Harold Sturdevant for one. He says you were in his house upsetting his daughter."

"I was in his house with his wife's permission talking with her daughter."

"Hal said she was crying."

"She was. Is he prepared to sign a complaint about it?"

"He don't need to sign a complaint."

"Sure he does," I replied. "If you receive any complaints, I'd be happy to review them with you and the Department of Public Safety when my license comes up for renewal."

The two big cops had been following our exchange with their heads, like sideline spectators watching tennis volleys. Now they had their heads toward Smollett, and Dexter was still examining his shoeshine.

Smollett changed neither his pose nor his expression. Just his voice grew strident. "I don't like wise-ass private detectives," he said.

My neck was actually getting stiff from looking up at them. There was a boulder nearby about knee high. I walked to it, sat down, and leaned back. The rock's surface was still warm from the June sun. "Maybe if we pooled our information on Stephen Kinnington, we could be more civil with each other."

Smollett began to tremble, his uniform hat rocking slightly over his head the way a pot lid does as the water boils beneath it. "Bring . . . him . . . up . . . here," he said, each word enunciated like a separate sentence.

The two big cops started sidestepping down immediately. Dexter reluctantly started down too. I said, "You know, Chief, there isn't a snowball's chance that Blakey could have identified that Mercedes that night."

Dexter and the big boys stopped dead and looked from me to the chief. Smollett said, "I said bring him up here," this time all in one sentence.

Just as the troops resumed their advance and I searched futilely for another delaying line, a car came barreling down Swan Street from the direction opposite the way I'd come. The troops halted again as Smollett looked over to the car. It stopped on the bridge and two car doors opened and closed.

"Afternoon, Will," said a welcome voice.

"Your car is blocking traffic," growled Smollett in reply.

Chief Calvin Maslyk's short, sturdy frame came into view. "Oh, there's never much traffic along here this time on a Saturday." A uniformed Bonham cop slightly larger than the biggest of Smollett's men loomed into view behind Cal. Maslyk looked down at me. "Afternoon, John."

"Chief," I said, smiling.

Cal didn't smile back, so I dropped mine.

"This is none of your affair, Cal," said Smollett, an officious tone replacing the angry one. "You're out of your jurisdiction."

Cal shrugged, unbuttoned a shirt pocket, fished for something in it. "Mr. Cuddy and I have a date at our pistol range. When one of my boys picked up Dexter's transmission to you over the radio, I thought I'd come out and pick him up for it." Maslyk found a cigarette and resumed his fishing, this time for a match.

"Since when did your men start monitoring *my* radio frequency?" snapped Smollett.

Maslyk smiled soothingly as he came up with his light. "Nobody was *monitoring* anybody, Will. One of the boys was just scanning and picked it up." Maslyk struck the match off his side-turned shoe. I hadn't seen that in years. "You know how it is, Will," said Maslyk as he cupped his hands around the match and tilted his face forward to light the cigarette.

Smollett fumed silently, then gestured to his troops with his head toward the cars. Dexter looked relieved and scampered back up. The two big ones looked disappointed and went sulkily back up, one stumbling to a knee to add insult, and dust, to injury. The four got into their cars, backed out, and gunned their engines down the road toward Meade.

I was sweating a bit more heavily than my flannel shirt and the rock's radiant heat could account for. "Thanks, Cal," I said quietly as I stood up.

"This time you were lucky. I can't have a man assigned to listen in on Smollett's transmissions, and hell, next time they'll use phones anyways."

I was halfway up the bank. "I agree," I said.

"This is not a good town for an outsider. Not when

he's poking into old deaths, important deaths." Cal waved his hand at the bridge and river.

"I agree," I repeated as I reached the top.

"So, you got any questions?" Cal asked.

"Just one," I said. "Where do you get those matches? They're impressive as hell."

Cal tossed his cigarette and stomped toward his car, jerking a hand for his driver to follow. "Goddamned wise-ass private eyes."

Twenty-First

SMOLLETT'S umbrage at my being in his town gave me a coward's way out for Val's dinner. I decided instead to drive there directly and settle things.

I turned into Fordham Road and stopped in front of Number 17. I climbed the steps and rang her bell.

"John!" It was barely five thirty, and she was dressed in a blue terrycloth robe. She threw her arms around my neck and hugged hard. She smelled of scented soap.

"Does tenure protect small-town teachers against charges of moral turpitude?"

She gave a little laugh and released her grip. Her eyes were bright as she smiled. "Just got out of the tub. You're early but I forgive you. Come in."

She took my hand and led me in. I swung the door shut. Her living room had a sunny bay window. Living in Back Bay and Beacon Hill, I'd grown used to fireplaces. There was none, but the room had a nice dining alcove under a beam near the kitchen. A half-closed door on the other side of the living room showed the foot of a bed.

She took me to the couch, and began talking as we sat down. "Aren't you dying in that heavy shirt?"

I wondered if I smelled rancid after the bridge encounter. "It's a little warm."

She released my hand and leaned forward to get up. As she did, her robe bowed forward and back. I was very much aware of her right breast and the tan line around it.

"Take it off," she said, smiling.

I blinked up at her. "Your shirt," she said, her smile growing broader, "take it off. I have a T-shirt that I use as a nightie that ought to fit you."

"No, thanks. Really," I said uncertainly. "I'm all right."

She planted her fists on her hips and looked resigned. "Well, if I can't make you comfortable, at least I can get you a drink. What will you have?"

"Orange juice," I said, and cleared my throat. "And a little vodka, if you've got it."

"I'll just be a minute," and she trotted off—to the kitchen for the drinks, not to the bedroom to change.

Well, John-boy, what now? Beth now. Beth and my decision. The question was how to put the decision into words. Or actions. And when. Something was beginning to make me perspire again. Maybe the flannel shirt.

She returned with the drinks. From across the room, mine appeared awfully pale. Unless she reconstituted her frozen o.j. with a lot of water, she'd mixed me a whale of a screwdriver. She handed it to me. As

140

she sat down, her robe did another calisthenic. I was positive she had known that it would.

"To lasting friendship," she said, with a nice try at a naughty wink.

I took a sip. Almost pure vodka. "You should hold the orange peel in a little longer next time."

She rolled the ice around in her glass and looked me up and down. "You know, John, you have a great sense of humor, but you shouldn't let it affect your taste in clothes."

We both laughed. "Actually, I'm on my way to find Stephen."

Valerie jumped forward and nearly spilled her drink as she set it on the coffee table. Her robe bowed out again and stayed that way. I kept looking into her eyes.

"Oh, John, you know where he is! Where?"

"I told Mrs. Kinnington I wouldn't tell her, and I'll not tell you for the same reasons. First, I'm not sure I do know where he is, and second, given Blakey's general temperament, I don't want anyone he could approach to know as much as I do."

Valerie shot me a disbelieving look. "Oh, come on, John. Blakey wouldn't dare try to intimidate me or Mrs. Kinnington."

"I don't mean to frighten you, but I'm not sure he wouldn't, if the stakes he's playing for are as high as I think they are."

She slid her hand onto mine. The hand was cold from her drink and warm from her at the same time. "I'm not frightened," she said.

I leaned away from her and against the backrest of the couch. My hand followed quite casually and naturally, and I interlocked my fingers in my lap.

Val turned sideways to me and brought her legs up

into a figure-four on the couch. She spoke in a whisper.

"From the way you're dressed and the things you've said, you expect to beat the bushes for Stephen somewhere. It'll be dark in another few hours. Do you really think that you'll find him at night?"

I cleared my throat again. "No, you're probably right."

She closed her hand over mine again. "I've got the chicken defrosted and some Sylvaner in the 'fridge. I can't promise you L'Espalier, but I can promise it will be nice." Another hard squeeze.

Now was the time. Instead, I lied. "That sounds good."

She leaned over, kissed me lightly on the cheek, and nestled her head into my shoulder. She also began stroking the back of my hand with the tips of her fingernails. She had long, pianist's fingers. and I noticed for the first time how long her nails were. I wondered how she could keep her nails so long, since she probably participated in vigorous school activities like recess. Then I remembered that school had been out for a while. Then I began to realize that I was thinking about her hands to avoid thinking about the lump in my throat. Now it was *really* time.

"Valerie . . . "

She arched her head back and up, her eyes half-open, her lips slightly parted.

"Val, it's just no good." I sat forward, and she drew back, her face an open cut.

"What . . . what do you . . . ?"

"Look," I said, more testily than I had a right to, "it's just not right between us. It just isn't there."

She began to look more mad than hurt. "What? What isn't there?" she demanded.

I began gesturing with my hand, making my points and waving her off at the same time. "A feeling isn't there. You're a nice person. A good human being. And being with you here so far has made me feel more warm than I have for months, since even before Beth died, because the last week or so she wasn't warm, she was just getting slowly colder, slowly slipping away. But that warmth isn't enough—there has to be something first, some kindred spark."

"So now," she snapped, "now you're going to say I don't 'spark' you? That you weren't excited to be near me?"

"No, that's not it. That's what's drawing me, don't you see? You're real, and you want me to be with you and be a part of your life. And that, plus the physical attraction, is what's drawing me to you. But I don't want to make you a part of my life. I don't feel toward you the way I felt toward Beth."

She threw her hands up and jumped to her feet. She crossed her arms and turned toward me and argued down to me.

"You big jerk! I'm sorry, John, but that's what you are. I can understand that I'm the first woman you've let yourself feel anything about since your wife died, and I can see why that would make you feel, oh, awkward even, like I think you've been tonight. But my God, John, how can you expect to feel toward someone the same affinity you felt toward Beth so soon? I mean, you knew her for, what, ten years? That's the sort of thing that takes time to grow, for God's sake!" Her eyes were filling with tears.

"But that's just it, Val. After Beth died, and in between binges with the booze, I read all sorts of articles, whole books even, on the need to rebuild, to start over in your life, block by block. The problem is, it's wrong. Those writers were wrong, and you're wrong. There really *are* special people in the world, people who are special to other people from the word go, and that's the way it was with Beth and me. She was the only woman I'd ever loved. She was the only one who knew me, who knew what I was thinking and could anticipate what I'd be doing. It was magic between us from the first time I met her."

"Magic?" Val said unbelievingly. "Magic?"

"Don't you see? I knew she was the one the instant I met her, and she did about me. Call it our Catholic upbringing or indoctrination if you like, but that was the attitude I had, and despite all the other Catholic attitudes I've fallen away from, it's still the one I have. And I'm right, Val. And the others, you, the writers and all, are wrong. At least about me."

Although Val then knelt in front of me, I'm sure she wasn't mocking my references to religion. She put her hands on my knees and leaned her face toward, and almost into, mine.

"John, that sort of thing does happen, but it happens when you're young, maybe when you're in high school or even college, before too many disappointments hit you and you wake up to the fact that life has imperfections in it. But you're ignoring reality if you tell me that unless it's love at first sight, a relationship can't work for you. That's just not the way it is, John."

I kissed her forehead and closed my hands over hers.

"I'm sorry, Val, but that's the way it is, at least for me. And if I kid myself any further about it, I really will be ignoring reality."

She blinked away her tears and rose to her feet. Her face took on a determined look.

"I feel sorry for you, John. I really do. Not because

your wife died, but because you're letting you die after her." She turned away and picked up the drinks. She began walking to the kitchen. "I'm afraid I'm going to have to retract the dinner invitation," she said over her shoulder.

I was already halfway to the front door.

As I drove away from Valerie's, I felt cold and empty. I just drove, paying little attention (to my eventual regret) to anything around me.

The problem was, Valerie was right about one thing: It was far too late in the day to begin looking for Stephen. I took a county road that wound roughly north. When it crossed Route 9, I headed west.

I came pretty quickly to the Sheraton Tara, a large, mock Tudor motor inn. It's about twenty miles from Boston where Route 9 and the Mass Pike intersect. I checked in, ate a monstrous steak in the restaurant, and then downed several too many screwdrivers while watching some suave suburbanites rock and disco till closing.

Twenty-Second

"Oh, I'm sorry, sir."

The maid was young and plain. She spoke with a heavy accent I couldn't catch. There was too much sunlight in the room.

She closed the door behind her as she backed out. I was on top of the covers of one bed, my pants on top of the other. I was still wearing my socks and flannel shirt. And my .38 in the calf holster. The air conditioner hummed at the window, and as I sat up I caught a glimpse of myself in the mirror over the low dresser-desk. Jack Lemmon in *Days of Wine and Roses.*

My watch said 11:35. Great. Real professional to get soused and not even leave a wake-up call.

I cleaned up, checked out, and was in my car heading west on the Pike by twelve-fifteen.

The Lee exit was about seventy miles west. The traffic was moderate for a Sunday, which in Massachusetts means three car-lengths at sixty-five miles per hour, despite the fifty-five-mile-per-hour limit.

The Berkshires sort of ease up on you, and they stay a little higher each mile westward as you drive into the valleys. I took the Lee exit and drove three miles north and two miles northeast to Granville.

I drove through Granville Center once, then turned around and parked near the church. A typical, small New England town. Catacorner from the church and across the common was a sporting goods–hardware–housewares store with front windows piled high with a mixture of plastic, wood, and iron items, more wood and iron than plastic. The front door's misplaced wind chimes tinkled a rhythmless ditty as I opened it. A head bobbed up from behind the counter.

"Aftahnoon."

I nodded in reply to the young clerk. Two years out of high school, probably the son of the owner. I was still decked out in my red flannel shirt with patch pockets, a pair of old Levi's, and boots. My .38 was strapped under the pantleg of my left calf. It was still a little too hot for the shirt.

"He'p ya?"

"Hope so. I'm interested in an old cabin a friend of mine in Boston saw advertised in the *Globe*."

He looked down a minute at the counter, lost in thought. It was glass top over old newspaper clippings of stringers of trout and deer hung for dressing, with the appropriate smiling sportsmen nearby.

"Ah don't read the *Globe*, but ah can't say as ah recall any cabin prop'ty 'round bein' fer sale." Most western Mass people do not have a New England accent, but this boy was a distinct exception.

I plunged on. "He said the ad mentioned an old ranger station."

The boy blinked and started rustling under the counter. He came up with an old topo map with a lot of pencil and pen marks on it. He spread it so we could both look at it if we turned sideways. He pointed to Granville's name on the map.

"We're heah." He moved his finger to a black box on a hilltop. "The station's theah." He next pointed to a perimeter road that went around the base of the hill. "Good road thcah." A spur road went up the hill toward the station. He pointed to the spur road. "Loggin' road'll get ya closer. Fah-wheel drive?"

I shook my head.

"Wahl, then, leave your vehicle at the base of the hill heah. The last four-five hunnerd yards you'll need to climb. More like hikin', really."

"Thanks," I said, and turned to go.

"On'y thing is," he said behind me, "no cabins t'all up theah."

"I'll check the ad, anyway."

No cabins. Nice cover, Cuddy.

I noticed him as I stepped into the sunshine. He was parked off to the side of the common in a different car than the one I'd seen before, probably a rental. He ducked his head into the magazine just a little too sharply when he saw me. My guess was, he had picked me up at Val's, possibly with Smollett's help. It would have been a cinch to tail me to the motel. Maybe he had even planted a transmitting bug in my car. No. No bug. More sophisticated than needed and probably beyond Blakey. I kept walking back to my car.

I got in and started up. I couldn't really fault myself for not noticing him behind me on the Pike. But I damn well should have spotted him thereafter and before I led him to Granville. I decided to drive around awhile to assess my options.

First, I could try to take him. I had my .38, but I had no justifiable reason to shoot him. I could fight him, but I'd never given away four inches and a hundred pounds before. Scratch Option One.

Option Two was to head back to the Pike and into Boston. No good. Even Blakey's minuscule mind would deduce that I wouldn't drive seventy-plus miles into the trees for the scenery. He might trail me to and even onto the Pike, but sooner or later he'd head back and ask the store clerk what I'd been up to, which would put Blakey between Stephen and me. Scratch Option Two.

Option Three was an extension of Option Two. I could drive to a decoy site, mess around for a while, then return in disappointment to my car and drive dejectedly back to Boston. The problem with Option Three was that as soon as he saw me heading back to Boston, he might still check in with the store clerk.

Enter Option Four. I could try to lose Blakey without allowing him to realize that I was trying. If I lost him, he'd go to the clerk. If he realized that I was trying to lose him, he'd come after me. I was willing to bet that he had the biggest engine allowed in his car, and could catch my four-cylinder Monarch in depressingly short order. There would follow a very unpleasant variation of Option One.

Option Five, the final one. I might be able to lead him close enough to the station without tipping him that I knew he was behind me. If I could keep the trail warm enough for him, I might (1) discourage his following me on foot and (2) delay his visit to the clerk. Option Five looked like the only choice.

I drove toward the ranger station but swung onto the perimeter road at the base of the mountain. The perimeter road was dirt and some gravel, and I threw a high rooster-tail of dry dust as I bounced along at a bone-crunching twenty or so. Blakey would realize that although my dust would hide him, I might see his dust if he drove too close. Since my slowly falling dust was a perfect trail of crumbs for him to follow, I figured he'd back way off and stay there.

I went by two long-abandoned camps and a house in ruins and executed a three-point turn so the car headed back the way it had come. I pulled it onto the shoulder and raised the hood. I then left my pack in the back seat with the windows open and lit out across the road and into the forest at the base of the mountain. I headed up as far as I could as fast as I could until I heard the sound of another car. Then I ducked down.

I couldn't see the road, but I could hear Blakey throttle down and then continue up the road at a low speed. I heard him fading in the distance for maybe a half mile; then he came back. He stopped near the car and turned off his engine. He probably checked my car and, seeing my gear still in it, figured I wasn't intending to be gone for long. He'd know that I hadn't had car trouble because I was facing back out the way I'd come in, a difficult maneuver if your car isn't working. He'd also figure, I hoped, that I'd intended it to look like car trouble so that if anyone did pass by, they wouldn't think a parked car was suspicious. I heard him reenter his car, start up, and move back down the road. I was willing to bet he'd angle in and hide it at the old house to wait for me to come down the road with Stephen. I then heard what sounded like a short spurt of reverse. Then his engine stopped long before it would have faded in the other direction. Good work, Option Five.

I continued up the mountain, approaching the ranger station from the back, blindside. With luck, Blakey would wait me out for a few hours. By that time, I'd have Stephen and we'd have arrived back in Granville after cutting across country the same way Stephen must have hiked in.

With luck.

Twenty-Third

ABOUT an hour later, I knew why the clerk had advised me to take the front road up to the ranger station. The grade on this side of the mountain was steep, the brambles sharp, and the bugs fierce. From the topo map, the ranger station was just over the crest. From the climb, I was still a good hour away.

When I reached and crossed the crest, I spotted the station. It was nearly sundown, but even in the fading light the box on stilts looked derelict. I waited and watched for half an hour. I then moved slowly to the base of the ladder of steps that connected the ground to the box sixty feet above. It was made of wood, and a couple of crossbars were missing. It would have been a hairy climb for a fourteen-year-old. I wasn't too enthusiastic myself.

I climbed the ladder, pulling myself by the arms rather than pushing myself by the legs. My hands I kept at the intersection points of the rungs with the vertical posts. A few groaned, but none gave way.

The ladder topped at a hatchway with a clasp long ago broken off. I raised the hatch and gingerly pulled myself up into the station.

It was a box perhaps thirty feet square, windows all around, but all broken. Bugs buzzed the hot air. An old desk, some debris from its official use, and some condoms and beer cans from its unofficial use. Otherwise, nothing.

Except for the floor. No broken window glass. And no dust. At least there should have been dust, and there should have been marks and scuffs in the dust from any recent users. No dust meant somebody had cleaned up. Cleaned up so the dust wouldn't show fourteen-year-old footprints. Just in case somebody came looking for him.

I walked to the front windows and looked down at the logging road. Then I walked to the back window and could see only the edge of the crest. The back side of the mountain must have been the responsibility of another station in the network. If I couldn't see Blakey, then he couldn't see the station. Fine.

The only other question was whether Stephen

would return before Blakey ran out of patience. I settled down to wait.

An hour. An hour and fifteen. An hour and twenty-five. I got up and looked out back. Nothing but deepening darkness. I walked to the front windows and, after crouching, eased my face to eye level and then slowly higher. I was about halfway up, when I heard a creak behind me and a voice that froze me.

"Don't move or I'll shoot you."

"Stephen, I'm—"

"Don't move! I have a twenty-two-caliber pistol pointed at you. I might not be able to kill you with it, but you'd never catch me or get down the ladder to a hospital in time. Now keep your hands on the sill and kneel down."

"Stephen—"

"Now!" His voice cracked.

I knelt.

He began to move in behind me. "Cross your one ankle over the other," he said.

"Your grandmother sent me."

He stopped. "Sure she did. Now cross your ankles and don't move while I search you. Okay?"

"Okay," I said. I crossed my ankles. It's almost impossible to pivot quickly on your knees that way. No problem, though. I figured I'd wait until I felt his hand on me, then disarm him.

He stepped slowly toward me. Then he must have broad-jumped and swung the pistol butt at my head as he landed. The room abruptly darkened to a midnight-blue fog.

I could taste the wool hairs in my mouth. I suppose

wool technically isn't hair, but when I was little, every night in the winter my brother and I slept in a rusty iron bed with a coarse woolen blanket over us. The cheaply made blanket would shed every night, and I'd awaken every morning with wool hairs in my mouth. I'd then feel waves of nausea coming over me and run to the bathroom with the dry heaves. One morning my half-opened eyes caught my brother putting the hairs in my half-opened mouth. I half-split his upper lip open with my fist.

I blinked my eyes, and I wasn't in my parents' house anymore. I was lying on my right side in the dark. Based on the ache from my right kidney, I'd been in that position for a while. I coughed and gagged. There was cloth in my mouth. I was also tied, hands (behind me) and feet. Taken and immobilized by a fourteen-year-old. I lifted my head, and John Phillip Sousa struck up the band at the back of my skull. I involuntarily bit into my gag, which I suspected was one or more wool socks. I coughed some more and flopped over onto my left side.

"Be quiet or I'll have to hit you again," came a low voice across the shadowy room.

"Ugglub caaam," I said.

"I mean it. We're not talking until morning when I can see your eyes."

I tried to recall if I'd mentioned Blakey. I couldn't remember, but I didn't think I would have risked it with a gun being held at my back by a boy who was terrified of him.

"Ercrue Baaka," I said. "Baaka, Baaka."

"Last warning," he said, his voice rising a little.

My head continued throbbing. I relaxed as best I could, and tried to forget about wool hairs and giant court officers. My left pant leg had been yanked out of my boot, and I could feel the empty holster on my calf. The throb in my head eased a bit, and I drifted off.

Twenty-Fourth

I realized the throbbing was gone. Then I heard a bird sing. Two birds. I opened my eyes, and it was full morning. Plenty of clean, bright sunshine in the room, but no Stephen.

I rolled up and went too far and keeled over onto my right side. The throbbing resumed. After a few more tries, I was sitting upright but hunched over. Stephen had run a connecting rope between my hands and my feet. I assumed he knew his knots. Walking, much less descending, the ladder was out of the question.

I edged backward until I could rest against the wall. I was hungry, but the thought of Blakey tracing my steps fast eroded my appctitc.

There was nothing I could see in the room that would help me get free. No sharp edges, no drawers I could reach. All the broken glass from the windows had been swept up by Stephen's cover-up. Which left the broken windows themselves.

I rolled onto my back and tried to stretch my legs. They were pretty numb, but even if they hadn't been, the rope connecting my hands and feet prevented me from stretching my legs high enough to reach the lowest of the broken windows.

I rolled back to a sitting position and tried to stand. No good. Feet and legs too numb. I squirmed and flexed until I could feel the pins and needles signaling the return of blood to my legs. Then I got a cramp in my left calf that left me munching on wool gag again. Finally, I edged my way up into a stooped position. I leaned back into the open window, but my hands behind me were still a good six inches from the sill. I didn't like the possible consequences of trying to assume a sitting position on the window shelf itself.

Then I heard the first footstep on the ladder.

I had never heard Stephen climbing the steps. But I was pretty sure he didn't weigh enough to make the room above shake the way it was.

A cross-piece gave way, and a muffled curse filtered up through the closed hatch. A minute later the hatch flew back and slammed as it hit the floor behind. The barrel of a .357 Magnum appeared, followed by the beefy hand holding it and the beefier face directing it. Blakey looked surprised when he saw me. Then he smiled. He came up one more step, sweeping the Magnum around the room. Then he pulled himself up, leaving the hatch open. He was dressed in now-dusty dark slacks and a light green shirt.

"Christ," he said, "am I glad to see you, asshole. Where's the kid?"

I did not dignify him with a reply.

"Aw, what's the matter? Kitty-cat got your tongue?" He holstered his gun and reached into his pocket as he came toward me. "Maybe this'll loosen things up a little."

He produced and opened a pocket knife. He cut the piece of rope around my head that was keeping the gag in place. Then he fished in my mouth with the blade and drew out the gag. A very damp gray sock. I could feel the wool hairs in my mouth but decided it would be impolite to spit. I swiveled my head and worked my jaws.

"Now," he said, "where's the kid?"

"He went out for Eggs McMuffin."

Blakey backhanded me on the left side of my face. I rolled awkwardly down the sill and banged my elbow hitting the floor. Blakey then kicked me hard in the back of my left thigh.

"I figure it's about sixty feet to the ground, wise-ass. A fall like that'd cover a lot of bruises."

My leg wouldn't work. "I don't know where he is, Blakey."

"I thought maybe he was gonna burn you at the stake, like a babysitter on TV."

I decided to try a smile. "He may yet."

Blakey smiled and crossed his arms, coplike. "You know, he's a fuckin' crazy kid. You know that."

"Then why do you want him back?" I asked, then clenched, fearing I'd unintentionally hit close to a nerve.

"What would I want him for?" he said warily. "It's the judge who wants him back. Back in the nuthouse where he belongs."

I unclenched and pursued the matter a little. "Then why all the cloak-and-dagger stuff? Why didn't the judge just let me help you find him?"

The smile passed. "None of your fuckin' business."

"Wouldn't have anything to do with a midnight swim four years back, would it?"

The lips curled back into a smile I didn't like. "The judge told you to stay out of this. The judge and me both. I warned you." His smile grew wider. "Remember?" he said huskily.

"I meant to tell you, you've got a sweet phone voice, pal."

Blakey stopped smiling. "This time the kid takes the blame. This time some local cop and I find you at the bottom of the ladder, with six slugs from the kid's twenty-two in you. Then I bring the kid to the nuthouse and call the judge. The judge takes it from there."

"Why not just kill the kid?" I asked, to gain some time.

Blakey laughed. "Boy, you are a cold-hearted bastard. I'll tell you why. It makes it tougher to explain why you're dead. And once I figured, sittin' by that broken-ass shed all night, that you'd spotted me, you had to get dead."

I thought I should argue that point. "What about the clerk in the hardware store? He can identify you."

Blakey unfolded his arms, and his face darkened. "How did you . . . ?" Then he laughed. "Oh, I get it. You figured out that's how I found you. Well, you're right, but that clerk won't know whether I found you here alive or dead."

I definitely didn't like his tone, but I was running out of deflections.

"Just in case you might try and warn the kid, you're gonna hafta go to sleep for a while. But first," he said, as he wrapped a handkerchief around his knuckles, "a little warm-up for your swan dive."

I got my left leg, the one he'd kicked, to bend a little. "I've got a secret about the kid that I'd like to share with you first."

"Nice try, asshole," he said as he cocked his fist.

"You think the kid'll climb up when he sees the open hatch?"

Blakey straightened up. He looked at the hatch and pursed his lips. "Maybe you're right." He ambled over and lowered the hatch. What I didn't mention was that Stephen, who must have made the climb a dozen times or more, sure as hell would notice the broken rung on the ladder. I was banking that with the hatch shut, Blakey wouldn't notice him noticing. Blakey walked back to me, and I tried to think of more episodes of the Arabian Nights. No luck.

"I've got another secret about Stephen," I said.

"What is it?" he replied.

"If I keep telling you secrets, will you keep me awake?" I thought about what Thom Doucette had said regarding Blakey's sensitivity.

"What the fuck is it?" he demanded.

"Well," I said, fluttering my eyelids, "Stephen told me that big, strong court officers really turn him on." Blakey bent down and gave me a wicked shot at the back of the right side of my jaw and front of my ear. The other side of my head bounced off the floor.

He then grabbed my shirt with both hands and lifted me to a semi-standing position. I'd known my only chance was to get him mad enough to treat me as harmless. He held my shirt with his left hand and let fly with his right. Before his fist could connect, I used his left hand as an anchorpoint and flipped back as violently as I could. With his left holding me, that brought my feet up toward his groin, and I lashed out with all the kick I could manage.

I cracked my head against the sill as I came down. My eyes wouldn't focus. I could see one and a half of him doubled over, with his three hands futilely trying to stem the spread of a dark stain at the crotch of his pants.

I shook my head as clear as I could and then levered onto my back. I swung my legs at his head and connected, but I got the impression that I'd only distracted him from his more immediate concern. As I flopped around, he swung backhand at my side, and I felt a rib break. The pain was incredible, and I prayed that it hadn't punctured a lung. Then he clouted me in the face with another backhand that sent me back into the sill. I could feel the room slipping away, and I knew I was going under. Then I heard a clacking noise, like a softball player opening a pop-top beer can. Then another and another and . . .

A tree fell and pinned my legs under it.

Twenty-Fifth

I couldn't move my legs, but I could rub them against each other a little. They felt sticky, as if ice cream had melted on them but hadn't quite dried. I opened the one eye that would open. The room was still light. The tree across my legs was Blakey. He was half on his side, and his blood had soaked through his pants. And mine.

His head was about fifteen inches from my eyes, but his face was turned away from me. The back of his neck looked funny. There were round, raw holes in it, two just above his hairline. It was as if someone had thrown large, blunt darts at him, darts that had first stuck in, then had fallen away. There was one down-

159

ward trickle of blood from each hole. I fell asleep again.

The next time I woke up, someone was pouring water into my mouth. Just a little. It tasted salty, probably from the dehydrated blood flakes in my mouth. I opened my eyes. It was nearly dark. Stephen was over me. Blakey was not in sight. Stephen's hands were dirty.

"Blakey?" I croaked.

"I took care of him," he answered.

I dropped back off to sleep.

I woke up to birds singing, light again, and more water. I felt weak but not much pain. Then I noticed that my hands were untied. I started to get up, and it felt as if someone set off an A-bomb in my left side. I stopped breathing and clenched my teeth. As I eased back down, so did the pain.

"Do you think you can handle some bread?"

He was behind me in the room. "Yes," I said.

"You won't try to grab me?"

"No."

"Okay."

I looked down at my feet. Still securely tied. Given my present condition, I figured about two undisturbed weeks would let me get the knots undone.

He came into my vision. He was wearing a polo shirt and loose-fitting hiking pants, cut like baggy army fatigues. He stopped three feet from me and lobbed a hunk of bread at me. It landed on Blakey's bloodstain, which had already dried. There were about ten ants nibbling at the edge of the stain.

"Still don't trust me, huh?" I said as I picked up the bread.

"Almost," he said.

In real life, he certainly appeared much older than fourteen. His face was somber and intelligent and his movements measured and sure, with none of the awkwardness of adolescence. There were still traces of blond in his dark hair, as though the sun were shining on him.

The bread crust grated against a newly chipped molar on the lower left side.

"How did you find me?" he asked.

I regarded my breadcrust and took another nibble, chewing on the other side of my mouth. I wanted time to review all the promises I'd made to people I'd spoken with, and my head wasn't reviewing as well as it might. "It's a long story," I said.

He hopped his bottom up on the desk and, crossing his ankles, swung his legs slowly to and fro under the desk top. "We've got time," he said without smiling.

"Well, I'm a private detective—"

"I know," Stephen interrupted. "I looked at your identification after I . . . while you were asleep."

"And, as I told you, your grandmother hired me to find you."

"How did *she* find *you*?"

I gave him my warmest reassuring smile. "Your teacher. Valerie Jacobs. Valerie knows me from an earlier job I had."

Stephen smiled back. A nice, good-kid type of smile. "Ms. Jacobs is a nice person," he said. "Go on."

"Well, from what you grandmother said, you hadn't been kidnapped. She knew that, she said, because only you or she could have handpicked your survival kit."

Stephen smiled more vividly. "Grandmother's

shrewd like that. I should have known she would guess."

I continued. "Once I accepted that you'd run away, I talked with your psychiatrist—"

Stephen's face darkened. "Which one?"

"Dr. Stein."

The smile returned. "He was kind of a jerk. I had the impression that he made a lot of money without really helping people much."

"Me, too," I said.

"Did he help you?"

"Not really," I said, trying to recall the chronology and not reveal anything I shouldn't. "But your stay at Willow Wood pointed me out this way."

He frowned. "I was afraid of that. But I didn't think going off someplace completely new would be a very good idea."

"That alone wasn't much help, but when Miss Pitts told me—"

"Boy," he exclaimed, "you went back as far as her?"

"Sure," I said. "I'm thorough."

"What'd she tell you?"

"About your mother's death."

Stephen darkened again and looked down. "I don't want to talk about that."

"Right," I said quickly. "Anyway, I thought it might have something to do with your disappearance, and I slowly traced you down through Ms. Moore at the library and—"

"Ms. Moore?" he said, quizzically. "What could she tell you?"

I explained about his copying the *New England Outdoors* article, including Ms. Moore's lingerie concerns. Stephen smiled sheepishly. "Did you check all the stations out before you hit this one?"

"No," I said. "I found out from Valerie that you had done a report on the meat distribution system, and then I had a . . . uh, little talk with the driver you hitchhiked with."

Stephen screwed up his face. "He was a pretty lousy guy."

I nodded.

Stephen unscrewed his face. "What did he tell you?"

I tried to keep old Sammy in and young Kim out "He said you had a gun. And that he would be laughed out of the meat exchange if anybody found out you'd taken him."

Stephen laughed, and I did too. Then he said, "I guess I wasn't as careful about coming out here as I thought."

"Well," I said, "neither was I."

Stephen tilted his head in question. "What do you mean?"

"Blakey. Following me out here."

Stephen shivered. "What made Blakey come after you like that?" he asked.

"I made a comment about his sexual preferences," I replied.

Stephen smiled sheepishly again.

"And yours," I added.

Stephen laughed innocently. "I'm still too young to have preferences."

"Then why did you shoot him?"

His smile froze. "Two reasons. One, he was killing you. Two, he helped the judge cover up the death of my mother."

"How?"

Stephen straightened up and walked away. "That's for me to speak with the judge about."

He arrived at the desk. He was packing his knapsack, his back toward me.

"Why did you run away?"

"Because I knew the judge would be after me. I found the proof."

I decided I'd better not even bend my promise to Kim. "What proof?"

"The twenty-two. The gun. The judge had hidden it the night my mother was killed. He'd hidden it so well that it took me till now to find it, but I knew I would. And I did."

"Then why didn't you go to the police?"

"Smollett?" He laughed oddly. "He helped cover up my mother's death."

"Your father killed her?"

"That's between us. Between the judge and me." He continued packing. I got the feeling we might better talk about the judge later.

"You going on a trip?" I asked.

"Yes. You, too."

"Where?"

"Back to Meade. To talk with the judge."

"Not without the county district attorney and maybe the state attorney general as well."

He left what he was doing and came around to squat on his haunches across from me.

"No, it'll just be you and me," he said. "I need you to drive me back. I was stupid to think that the judge wouldn't send people after me. After I found the gun, the judge must have realized it, he must have checked on it when I wasn't around. He probably checked it every day because of what it could do to him. He sent

164

Blakey after me, and I panicked and ran. Blakey's dead, but he'll always send people after me. If Blakey could trace you here a day after you arrived, then somebody else knows about this place and can come back here after me. And every other place I try to go."

Something jangled. Something wasn't right, but I still couldn't pull it together. Then I thought about Blakey talking to the hardware clerk. Blakey had probably called the judge then, before he came out here again. I would have. So the judge would know about the hiding place.

"Why should I drive you? Because otherwise you'll shoot me?"

Stephen got somber again. He stomped over to his knapsack and came stomping back. I held my breath, but he tossed the knapsack down in front of me. "No more guns! I buried them! Go ahead and search it!"

I hefted the knapsack, then pawed through it. No weapons.

"Then I repeat, why should I drive you anywhere?"

He grinned. "Because of three things. One, I dragged Blakey out of here and down the hatch. I rolled him, really, across the floor with a rope around his belt, but I don't think anybody would believe I had the strength to do it. He hit the ground below us. Then I pushed him until he rolled into some soft weeds downhill. Then I buried him.

"Two, I took the twenty-two, wiped it off, and then put it in your hand. I squeezed your fingers around it and even fired a shot with your finger around the trigger. Then I buried the gun in a different place than I buried Blakey.

"Three," and he smiled broadly at this, "I hiked into town and mailed my grandmother a letter, describing how I saw *you* do all this."

I expect I failed to maintain a poker face. "I don't believe you."

His smile faded. "Then don't drive me anywhere. I'll be leaving soon. Eventually I'll be able to hitch a ride back to Meade. Meanwhile, I'll take the car keys with me, and I don't think you can hike out, hurt like you are. That leaves you to wait for the police. If they get here before you die from hunger or thirst."

"The police won't be coming."

"Oh, yes, they will," he replied. "My grandmother will call them when she gets my letter."

"You didn't write any letter."

"Yes, I did. But even if I didn't, I could still be gone and call the police before you could do anything about it. Or not call the police and leave you here to die."

I leaned back and faked a grimace to think it over. In his own organized way, Stephen had to be crazy, Dr. Stein to the contrary notwithstanding. Whether he had sent the letter or not, my past run-in with Blakey at the courthouse, combined with the hardware clerk's identification, would tie me in to his death. If Stephen had sent the letter or made a call, I doubted that I'd be allowed out on bail to try to find him to explain things. Especially if he had made his letter sound as if I might kill him, too. I decided that I'd better agree to drive him before he figured out how to drive himself. "If I do drive you back to Meade, can I go to the hospital?"

He brightened. "After we talk with the judge. I want you there." Then the brightness drained from him. "Without a gun, and without you there, I'm afraid he'd kill me."

Twenty-Sixth

STEPHEN told me that he'd found Blakey's rental car at the base of the trail up the front of the mountain. Stephen advised me, however, that the hood was up. I told him that it was an old trick and that I was sure the car would work. Besides, I knew I couldn't go back down to my car the way I'd come up, or even by walking along the perimeter road.

My face was pretty much numb, but my rib was killing me. Stephen cut my ankle bonds, and I found after a while that I could still walk, at least around the room.

I had some canned fruit cocktail and some dry chocolate candy with almonds. Stephen wanted to leave so we could arrive in Meade at approximately 9:30 P.M. I told him that in my condition I wanted to complete the downhill part of the trip while it was still bright outside. He agreed.

We started down. The ladder was the worst part of the ordeal. On the trail, I asked Stephen to help support me a few times, which gave me the opportunity to frisk him unobtrusively. He wasn't carrying any weapons.

We got to Blakey's car just at sunset. I lowered the

hood. It started on the second try, and Stephen rewarded me with a smile.

I had to take the dirt road very slowly. Once on the paved road back to the Pike, we stopped at a supermarket. A sign in the window read "Closed all day tomorrow, July Fourth." Stephen went in to buy me some more bread. While he was gone, I did another quick search of his knapsack. Clean.

Stephen got back in, and we continued on to the Pike. I asked him if he thought the judge would be at home, since the next day was a holiday.

"Sure," he said. "He always gives a big speech after the parade. He'll be home tonight, practicing it like every year."

Then we talked about Valerie, camping, and the army. He knew a lot about the service, obviously from reading up on his Uncle Telford and what he had done. I judiciously avoided my visit to Kim Sturdevant's house.

I've never been much for kids. Even when Beth was alive, I was perfectly happy to borrow somebody else's kids when Beth and I acted as free babysitters for the afternoon. Then, having had my fill, I could return them at night, like short-term library books.

Stephen, though, was different. He truly appeared to be a gifted, sensitive boy. I tried to square that with how he had handled Blakey. I decided that his maturity and intelligence might have permitted him to shoot Blakey to save me, but I couldn't account for his disposing of Blakey's body in such a way as to gain leverage over me. He was, I suppose, one of the few individuals, child or adult, who interested me more the more I came to know him.

On the well-maintained roads, I began to forget

about my rib. Over two hours later, as we turned in to the Kinnington driveway, however, the lurch onto gravel brought tears to my eyes.

I braked the car to a halt, but not because of my rib cage. There was a heavy double chain stretched across the driveway. The chain was anchored at both ends by short, stout metal poles.

"I don't remember this from my earlier visits," I said.

Stephen was staring at the chain. "That's all right. There's another way. In fact, it's a better way."

I sighed and gingerly shifted to face him. "Stephen, what kind of way is it?"

"It's a path, on the other side of the hill. It leads up to the back of the house."

"Can we drive the car up it?"

Stephen turned to me. "No, but it's shorter than climbing up this driveway." I frowned, but Stephen continued quickly, "No, really! It'll be a lot easier on you, I promise."

I nodded. He said, "Back the car up and keep going down the road like we were."

I followed his instructions. As we drove, I asked Stephen why rich people's driveways weren't paved. He said the judge felt that paved driveways encouraged passersby to drive up them and that gravel driveways did not. Also, gravel drives were more genteel and therefore more in keeping with the "overall Kinnington environment." It must have been a great environment for the poor kid, I thought.

We slowed about half a mile after the driveway and took a right onto a narrower but still paved road. At Stephen's direction, I pulled to a stop near an old stone fence marker.

"This is it," he said.

I eased out of the driver's side, but Stephen stumbled in the dark and into some bushes as he was swinging open the door.

"You all right?" I whispered.

"Yes," he said. "Just a few scratches."

I could hear him scuffling back up to the car and gently closing the door. We left his knapsack in the car. The crickets were chirping madly, and there was a scent of freshly mowed grass in the warm, heavy night air.

"Come on over here," he said from the other side of the car. "The path is right here."

I moved around to the back of the car and fumbled with Blakey's keys at the trunk as my eyes tried to adjust to what night vision the moon would allow me.

"What are you doing?" asked Stephen.

"I'm checking for a flashlight. Look in the glove compartment, will you?"

"Don't bother. I searched the car at the ranger station. There's no flashlight."

I pocketed the keys and reminded myself that things would probably progress faster if I left the lead to the genius.

I was pretty stiff from our drive as we started up the path. The moon was just bright enough to allow me to see where I was walking. The path was only two feet wide, but some worn spots indicated it used to be wider. Stephen obviously was at ease climbing it, partly youth and partly familiarity.

"Did you clear this path yourself?" I whispered.

"No," he laughed softly, getting a few steps ahead, then waiting for me to catch up. "The men who cleared the underbrush and deadwood from the grounds here used this because it was easier than carrying the stuff up past the house to the driveway. My uncle and my father used to play on it as kids, too."

I stopped and looked around. Even in the weak light, I could see a lot of brush intruding on the trail and deadwood along side of it. "Looks like it's been a while since the landscapers have been around."

Stephen's voice had no laughter in it now. "It has. The judge and Blakey do . . . did what there was to be done."

I looked at him quizzically, but in the moonlight I couldn't read his face and he probably couldn't see mine. "Your grandmother told me that you have over seventy-five acres here. Why the hell doesn't your father have someone come to take care of this stuff?"

Stephen turned up the trail. "You'll see," he said flatly as I began after him again.

I tried to go slowly, on the theory that the less frequently I had to breathe, the better my ribs would feel. After about five minutes of climbing, however, the throbbing pain was distracting me and increasing with every step.

I noticed I was focusing my eyes on the ground. Not just the path under me, but the yard or so in front of me as well, my head bobbing slightly. That snapped me back for a moment to Vietnam. When I was there, MP lieutenants were shuttled into infantry platoons if the infantry companies were short of young officers. I hated patrols in the jungle, or "the bush" as the troops called it, and I was terrified of land mines, which killed or maimed so unpredictably that they would have seemed whimsical in a less personal setting. The Cong would stretch thin wire across the trails as trips for the mines. You bobbed your head to vary the moonlight hitting the path ahead of you in the hope that a change in the angle of light and sight would pick up a stretched wire that the point man might have missed. It had been a long time since I had been reminded of that, and I hoped it would be a longer time before the memory surfaced again.

Lost in thought, I nearly fell over a stone or maybe an exposed root in the path. I cursed under my breath as I stumbled and my rib shrieked.

"Are you all right?" whispered Stephen, just ahead and out of sight.

"Just a few scratches," I mimicked.

He laughed softly again and urged me on.

Just as I thought I would have to call a rest, Stephen let me catch up to him on the trail. "We have to go off the path a little ways here."

"Why?"

"You'll see," he said, turning into the brush.

"Stephen, wait a minute," I said. I leaned back against a tree to ease the pressure on my breathing apparatus. "I'm hurting pretty badly. Detours are not a happy prospect right now."

His voice dropped very low, so low I could barely hear him, even in the summer stillness. "I want you to believe me. I want you to see this before we see the judge. Please, it's important. Please?"

"See what, Stephen?"

"Please?"

I sighed. "How far?"

"Not far," he said quickly. "Maybe twenty yards. He couldn't . . . Maybe not even twenty."

I told my rib that the kid had been through a lot. "All right," I said. "But let's take it real slow and easy, okay?"

"Sure. Slow and easy."

"Real slow and easy," I corrected.

"Right," he said, and we slipped under a branch and began edging in.

We had moved about his twenty yards when he stopped and sank slowly down to his knees.

"This is it," he said, looking down but not otherwise moving.

I eased down on one knee. There was a decaying log with a large clump of wildflowers growing around it. "What is it?" I asked quietly.

"Her grave," he said. "My mother. This is where he buried her."

I had nothing to say. I looked at Diane Kinnington's place and I thought of Beth's place. Both were on hillsides, and both had flowers. And each, it seemed, had one faithful mourner.

"I was there when he shot her," Stephen said in the low, flat voice. "It was . . . " He stopped. Then, "Afterwards, he locked me in my room. The judge had hit me, knocked me out, I guess, but I woke up. I heard him, through the window, at the tool shed. I got up and looked out, but it was too rainy and dark to see well. The judge was carrying some tools, I could hear them clanging together, and he was hurrying down the path with them. I must have passed out then, because the next thing I remember is being in an ambulance on my way to Willow Wood and nobody would listen to me."

"They'll listen now," I said, forgiving his failure to remember that he had been catatonic. I restrained myself from patting his shoulder. He was only fourteen, but he didn't seem to need any comforting.

Stephen continued. "When I was at Willow Wood, I

had time to think." He changed his voice and said, " 'All the time in the world'," as though he were mocking a doctor's phrase there. "I figured out what must have happened, but I couldn't tell anyone about the judge covering it up. Who'd believe me against him? When my grandmother got me out of Willow Wood, I came home and acted like nothing . . . like the judge hadn't done anything. I was afraid to tell my grandmother, afraid that he'd kill her too. When I could, I searched. I had to be really careful. I searched for the gun, and finally found it. But first I had to search . . . for her."

The ache was getting me, so I shifted knees. Stephen tensed when I moved, then relaxed and settled from his knees onto his haunches. He had yet to look away from the grave. "I had to be sure the judge didn't realize I was searching, so I didn't do it every day, sometimes not even for a week. It was tough not to, but it was a quest, and I couldn't let her down by being discovered. I knew from what I saw at the window that he had buried her somewhere down the path. But it had been almost a year, and I didn't know if he would have dug . . . moved her, moved her while I was away at Willow Wood.

"Then one day I found this spot. I remembered the fallen tree from a storm we'd had that year. But the tree didn't look right, and I realized it was because of all the flowers. There were flowers other places, but there hadn't been any here and now there were lots and lots of flowers, but mostly in this one little spot. At first I thought that God had put them here special, special for her and special for me so I could find her." He rubbed his right forearm across his eyes. I found myself doing the same.

"Then I read in a botany book that flowers grow over bodies that aren't . . . in coffins. That's when I was sure she was here. I came to visit every day, but I'd walk in from a different direction each time, so as not to make a path that would let the judge know I'd found her. Some days, I wouldn't even come right up to her, because I didn't want the plants around her to look trampled." He finally swung his face toward mine. "Did you ever have anybody close to you be buried?"

I hadn't stopped thinking about Beth since he'd begun. "Yes," I said in a choked voice.

He tried to examine me in the moonlight. "You're crying," he said. He looked back down at the grave. "I'm ready to see the judge now," he said.

So was I. So . . . was . . . I.

Twenty-Seventh

HE'LL probably be in the library," Stephen whispered as he beckoned me toward the back of the house.

"Does the house have an alarm system?" I asked, still winded from my hike up the path.

"Yes," he said as we approached the back door, "but he never turns it on until he goes to bed."

Stephen produced a key, and we entered the house. I followed him to a turn in the corridor. He took the turn, and we approached two large polished double doors.

Stephen looked up at me. "Ready?" he whispered.

"Does he keep a gun at his desk?" I asked.

Stephen shook his head. "Only upstairs, in the bedroom."

"Then I'm ready."

We opened the doors.

The judge was standing in front of a mirror. He was dressed in an Izod Lacoste sport shirt and khaki pants. He had notes in his hand and appeared to have been rehearsing his speech. "Practicing a eulogy?" I asked.

He looked at us as if we'd entered the Debutante's Ball naked.

"Sit down, Judge. We want to have a little lobby conference."

The judge looked over at the telephone. Stephen briskly walked over to the wall and pulled the plug from the wall jack. The judge moved unsteadily toward his desk chair. I took an easy chair and tried to maintain my smile as I lowered my ribcage into it. Stephen sat to my right and a little behind me, keeping me between him and his father.

It was a beautiful room, with carefully polished wainscoting and natural-wood bookshelves. I would say "restored" wood, but I doubt that that particular wood had ever been allowed to deteriorate. The books I could see were mainly law titles, with some leather-bound, gold-lettered fiction classics by Defoe, Dickens, and assorted others sprinkled around.

The judge slumped into his chair and then tried a fine, arrogant recovery.

"Mr. Cuddy, I must say I underestimated you. I want to thank you for returning Stephen to me."

"Aren't you even curious about Blakey?" I asked.

The judge lost a bit of his regained color. "What about him?"

"He didn't fare too well after he called you yesterday."

The judge started, then must have inwardly cursed for thus confirming my suspicion about the call.

"What did he do, Judge, happen on you as you dumped your wife in the river?"

The judge tried a snarl that queerly came off as a smile. "I don't know what you're talking about. I intend to call—"

"Or more accurately, as you dunked your wife's car?"

The judge lost his queer smile.

"Where did you bury her, Judge?" I asked.

"We know," said Stephen. His voice was very flat.

The judge looked from me to Stephen and back to me.

"Officer Blakey will deny every one of these ridiculous . . ."

I leaned back farther in my chair.

Stephen said, "Blakey's dead." Still the flat voice.

The judge jerked violently.

"That's what I meant by eulogy when we came in," I added.

The judge said, "Blakey wasn't there. Blakey only helped me afterwards. After he—"

"It's too late to deny things," said Stephen, changing his inflection to a sing-song, as though he were the adult explaining the world to a dull child. "I told Mr. Cuddy everything."

The judge's eyes went wide in terror. "Where's the gun?" he whispered to me, like an aside in a Shakespeare play.

177

"The twenty-two?" I asked.

"Yes, yes!"

"Why?" I asked.

"Because it's the one thing that can clear me, you idiot! I thought he'd been cured after he came back from Willow Wood. I couldn't have the publicity, the madness in the family and all. I wanted to be elevated to the superior court, but I had to protect myself. The gun had his fingerprints on it. I hid it so well, I thought he'd never find it—so well I thought he'd given up looking for it." Then turning to Stephen: "But you never did, did you? You found it, and I realized it and Blakey missed you, and you ran, you little bastard. I authorized the absolute minimum search possible. I prayed to God that some hobo would slit your throat in a ditch."

"Judge, maybe if you told me what—"

"I *have* to tell you, can't you see that? Now that Blakey's dead, I have to." He was becoming unglued. Stephen remained silent.

"After she wouldn't shut up that night, drunk and vile as she was, about how much she'd enjoyed making love with Tel, about how much she'd enjoyed having his baby and making me act the father, then after he was born, him being so much like Tel, even down to the . . . Ah, but he didn't tell you that part, did he? *Did* he!"

I began to feel weak in the gut. I glanced back at Stephen. He was staring straight ahead, his face unsmiling but his eyes twinkling.

I turned back to the judge. "Tell me what?"

The judge began to shake. "Where's the gun?" he demanded.

"Stephen buried it. After he killed Blakey with it."

The judge shook more violently.

"Did you see him bury it?"

"No."

"Dear God, first his mother, now Blakey, and I can't—"

"Are you trying to tell me that Stephen—"

I heard the zipper sound but didn't turn immediately. By that time Stephen had my .38 out of the crotch of his pants and leveled at the judge. He must have hidden it under the passenger side of the front seat when he found Blakey's car at the ranger station and then retrieved it when he "stumbled" out of the car at the beginning of the path.

In my peripheral vision I caught the judge standing up too quickly as he yanked open the middle drawer in his desk, banging his knees on the drawer as he did so. Then the first shot. The bullet knocked the judge back into a bookcase niche with a brandy decanter and cut-crystal liqueur glasses and brandy snifters. Stephen probably was not used to the greater kick of the more powerful weapon. His second shot ruined a painting above the niche.

My rib was screaming at me as I dived at Stephen, my left fist aimed at his face. He ducked as he swung the barrel toward me. The blast deafened me. I felt a sledge hit my left shoulder. The follow-through sent me into Dreamland.

Twenty-Eighth

I'VE always suspected that patients could go snow-blind in hospitals. They are some of the very few semipublic buildings that are still glaring white and usually clean.

The last few times I'd opened my eyes, I'd been surrounded by blurry, white-furred polar bears growling and grunting and poking at me. Now I could narrow my focus down to a nurse and a doctor. The doctor spoke first.

"Can you hear me, Mr. Cuddy?" she asked.

"No," I replied.

The doctor mumbled something to the nurse, who nodded and left the room.

"Do you have any pain?"

"Doctor," I said as sweetly as I could, "a gunshot wound always produces a numbing effect."

She smiled. "With your problems, you'd better be nice to me. The schoolteacher and I seem to be the only friends you've got right now."

"Why is that?"

"I've been told not to talk with you."

"Then send Valerie in."

"If that's the schoolteacher, I can't."

"Why."

"District attorney's orders."

"Oh." A bad sign. I turned my head. There was a cop with a notepad sitting on a chair in the corner and scribbling furiously. Otherwise, no other people. Nor any other beds. There were some trees outside the window.

"If I've been here more than ten minutes, this private room has bankrupted me."

The doctor laughed. "The county's paying the tab."

Another bad sign. A very bad sign.

I tried to hunch up in bed. The doctor stifled a smile as I yelled. The cop jumped up. The doctor placed her hand lightly on my left shoulder as I decided lying down was a very good position to maintain. The cop looked at his watch, sat down, and returned to scribbling.

I couldn't remember how hard I'd hit Stephen. As far as I could tell, my memory was otherwise intact.

"How's the boy?"

"The Kinnington boy?" she said. "He's doing quite well. The X rays say a broken jaw, but he'll be going home soon, and—"

"Home!" I thundered as the door burst open. The cop half-rose and reached for his gun. Through the door came Stanley Brower, the district attorney of Norfolk County. Behind him in the corridor I could see the Boston-area version of the paparazzi pushing in on a small barricade of police officers. A young man who looked a year or so out of law school followed Brower in.

Brower gave the cop a dirty look and a beckon. The cop released his gun. His notepad fluttered as he followed Brower and his assistant into a corner of the room. The assistant clicked on a tape recorder as the cop mumbled heatedly. Brower asked a question, got a negative shake of the head from the cop, and disgustedly waved him back to his chair. The DA spoke briefly to his assistant, and then they approached my bed.

"Mr. Cuddy. I am Stanley—"

"I know who you are, Mr. Brower. What's this I hear about the Kinnington boy going home soon?"

Brower waited for my interruption to cease. "Mr. Cuddy, you have the right to remain silent. If you speak, anything you say—"

". . . can and will be used, and I can have an attorney, or one will be appointed for me if I can't afford one, thanks to Messrs. Miranda, Escobedo, and Gideon. Now why are you releasing the Kinnington boy?"

Brower regarded me. "Why are you so interested in him?"

"Mr. Brower, I will be happy to speak to you on a number of conditions. Condition number one is that Tommy Kramer be in the room with a stenographer of his choice. The other conditions will be explained to you when he arrives."

Brower thought it over. Kramer, the lawyer I had called about my Empire firing, was the most respected attorney in the city of Dedham, the Norfolk County seat. "Kramer doesn't do criminal work, Mr. Cuddy."

"I know," I replied. "No lawyer's going to persuade you that I didn't do whatever it is you think I did. I just want a fair witness present."

Brower spoke to his assistant. "Call Tom Kramer and see if he'll come down."

"I want you here when he arrives," I said. "Meanwhile, I'd like lunch. Or is it still breakfast?"

"Early supper," said Brower as the doctor hit the nurses' call button at the side of my bed. "But I'm afraid you missed the July Fourth barbecue. You've been unconscious for a day and a half."

Tommy Kramer came into the room with a young woman carrying a stenographer's case. The cop relinquished his chair, and she set up. When she nodded to Tommy, he said, "Stan, I'd like to speak to Mr. Cuddy alone first."

"No," I said. "I want everyone here to realize that I'm speaking without advice of counsel."

"John, I have to advise you—"

"No, Tommy, I'm being set up, and not by Mr. Brower's office. My only conditions beyond your presence and your stenographer's taking notes are one, that nothing of what we say will be off this record, two, that I will be allowed to speak in a narrative style instead of answering questions, and three, that nothing we say will be communicated to any of the Kinnington family by anyone except you, Mr. Brower."

Kramer looked at Brower. Brower said, "Agreed." Kramer looked at the young lawyer with the tape recorder. Kramer said, "Stan?"

Brower sighed. He looked at the kid and said, "Doug, leave the room."

The young DA started to open his yap, then closed it. He handed the tape recorder to Brower.

"You, too," said Brower to the cop.

"The chief told me—"

"I said leave," said Brower in the same tone.

The cop and Doug left. Brower had each of us identify ourselves and our voices for the tape. He gave
background on time, place, and purpose. It was the
investigation into the deaths of Blakey and the judge.

"I assume that you've spoken with Stephen, and he
has told you that I killed Blakey or the judge."

Brower said, "The boy told us you killed both."

I drew a long breath. "Stephen is lying. Stephen is
psychopathic. He was institutionalized in a
sanatorium four years ago after he shot his mother to
death. The judge covered it up to protect his own
ambitions and got Blakey to help him in it. Stephen
killed Blakey and the judge. Stephen's insane, but has
an incredible intellect, and he therefore must be
examined by at least three of the smartest psychiatrists you can find, because I'm betting he'll fool at
least one. What I want to do now is tell you what
really happened."

I then droned on for more than two hours, going
through the entire chronology of the case, both before
and after I entered it. When I wasn't sure what really
happened, I stated that I was assuming facts. The
only parts I deleted were my meetings with Nancy
DeMarco in the bar and with Thom Doucette in the
park, and I also held back a few of Kim's statements.

"Therefore," I concluded, "it is vital that you protect the following pieces of real evidence: Stephen's
fingerprints on the plastic phone jack in the judge's
library, his fingerprints on the wooden handle of my
thirty-eight, the pistol-oil traces that have to be on
the inside of the crotch of his pants and have to match
the oil from my thirty-eight, the trajectory paths of
the bullets in the judge and in the wall, which will
show they were fired from Stephen's chair, not mine,

and these," I said, extending my hands. "The rope burns on my wrists. And ankles. Add these to the fact that with a broken rib I could never have handled Blakey. Add them to the fact that if I were going to kill Blakey and the judge, I'd need a motive. And if I were going to kill them, tell me why I'd try to pin it on a fourteen-year-old and do such a damned poor job of it."

Brower had sat at the foot of my bed about fifteen minutes into my monologue. He listened with his arms folded across his chest.

"Are you finished?" he asked.

"Yes." I was fighting my sleep reflex.

Brower made some concluding remarks for the tape and the stenographer. Then he turned off the tape, and the stenographer disassembled and exited.

Brower looked at me, then at Tommy. "Two days I've been chewing on this case," Brower began. "No motive for Cuddy past a routine pissing contest with Blakey, an angelic little kid with a home life like a soap opera, guns galore, deputies digging by a ranger station in the forest, and a flower bed Stephen told us about behind his house. It didn't add up, but I had to be awfully right before I acted. I couldn't afford to be wrong here. Not with this family."

Brower turned to me. "Nancy DeMarco called me just before lunch and told me she'd talked to you, and she corroborated enough of what you just told me. She's also bringing me a letter that she says she received from you, spelling out where you were going and why. Not the sort of thing a murderer precedes his crimes with. Cal Maslyk called me with similar support. I did enough other checking on you to be pretty sure you wouldn't be doing something like this.

Keep in touch for testifying." Brower headed for the door.

"By the way," I said, "Nancy DeMarco is likely to be in the job market soon. You'd do well to give her a shot with your office."

Brower squared himself to face the press and replied over his shoulder. "Thanks, Cuddy, but I didn't get where I am today by following staff advice from private eyes who get taken by fourteen-year-olds."

I looked over at Tommy, who'd been sweating bullets and would probably never forgive me.

Twenty-Ninth

THE good doctor advised me that my marathon with Brower had weakened me so that she wouldn't release me for another day. She also instituted some sort of sedative-painkiller for the hole in my shoulder. The nurse gave it to me, then said, "The schoolteacher is here to see you. I told her you'd be sleeping again in about fifteen minutes."

"Send her in." The nurse left.

Valerie edged in. We exchanged the sort of pleasantries you hear at high school reunions between acquaintances who don't see anyone else to talk to. There really was nothing there for her, and she sensed it. She left. I drifted off.

Something woke me. The nurse stuck her head in the door. "Still awake, bright eyes?"

"Yeah."

"More visitors."

"Do they have an appointment?"

She looked behind her. "One of them has probably never needed one."

I blinked my eyes. "Send her in."

The nurse beckoned over her shoulder and held open the door as Mrs. Kinnington came in, crablike on her braces. Mrs. Page followed and arranged a chair near my bed. Mrs. Kinnington leaned the braces against the side of my bed. The housekeeper gave me the same look she'd greeted me with that first day and then exited with the nurse.

"Mr. Cuddy, you accomplished that which no one else was able to do. For that I am grateful."

"Much better, thank you for asking."

She dropped her eyes to her purse and opened it. "Couldn't we eliminate the sarcasm? My grandson is and has been all that has mattered to me. I am sorry you were injured, but"—and she extended a check to me—"I am sure that this will cover all expenses and fees."

I took it and folded it without looking at it. "I'm sure it covers even the speech I'm about to make. Mrs. Kinnington, there was never anything between Blakey and your grandson, was there?"

"I certainly hope not, but as I explained to you, I have no way—"

"Mrs. Kinnington," I interrupted, 'I'll cut the sarcasm if you'll cut the bullshit. That 'relationship' was something out of Miss Pitts's imagination that you fanned."

"I've no time to listen to raving." She reached for her braces. I got them first and flung them into the corner. My left shoulder seared, then simply throbbed as they clattered against the wall.

"You unspeakable bastard!"

"I'm sorry, Mrs. Kinnington, but I'm not finished yet. Stephen is a very sick boy in a whole lot of trouble."

"If you mean that pack of nonsense that Brower man . . ."

"It is no nonsense, Mrs. Kinnington," I said. I found I had to keep my eyes closed. "Your grandson has by my unofficial count violently killed three people, two in my presence. The third was his mother after she drunkenly provoked him by telling him he was illegitimate. Your grandson may be an intellectual prodigy, Mrs. Kinnington, but he desperately needs professional help. For his mind. And not just Willow Wood and arts and crafts and canoeing." Mrs. Kinnington did not answer for a moment. I kept my eyes closed. She broke first.

"Stephen has told us that you killed Blakey. Stephen has told us that the judge killed his mother. Stephen has also told us that the judge was reaching for the gun in the desk drawer. That's why you shot him."

"Mrs. Kinnington, the DA doesn't believe that and neither do you. Stephen does not know right from wrong. He doesn't understand what lying is, and he doesn't understand that most killing is wrong. Just like his father."

"I won't have that kind of talk about Stephen or my son."

"Which son do you mean?"

"I don't intend to listen—"

"Mrs. Kinnington, you damn well will listen. While I was lying here, thinking this through, something finally hit me. Stephen had *planned* to go to that ranger station. Hell, he had photocopied the article after he found the gun, but *before* Miss Pitts saw Blakey chasing him. It took me a while to figure that out, but you should be able to see where it leads. Stephen planned to take off, maybe hoping the judge himself would follow to somewhere that Stephen could control the action. Blakey's chase was just the immediate trigger for Stephen's leaving."

"I refuse—"

"Look," I interrupted again. "When I found him at the ranger station, your grandson couldn't chance believing that I was working for you. He figured that I might have had a partner with me, so he checked around the ranger station and eventually must have spotted Blakey. Your grandson then left me tied up to lure my 'partner' Blakey. Then Stephen 'happened' to get back in time to see us fighting and drill about six well-placed holes in the back of Blakey's neck and wrap my hand around the gun. Stephen would have killed me then too, if he hadn't needed me to—"

"I will not—"

"Shut up or I will shut you up. Stephen figured I was busted up enough so that he could take me back at your house after using me as the fall guy for killing the judge. With my own gun. But I was able to knock Stephen cold before he could properly arrange the frame and before he could finish me off in his 'struggle' with me after I allegedly shot the judge before his horrified, sheltered, fourteen-year-old eyes. And because he couldn't arrange the frame properly, there are half a dozen facts that he can't change, facts that point to him as damningly as holding the proverbial smoking gun."

"The judge persecuted Stephen because he was afraid of him. My grandson will never go to trial." She was yelling now.

"Mrs. Kinnington," I said softly, "your grandson will go to trial, unless the DA's psychiatric experts testify that he is unable to stand trial by reason of insanity."

Somebody started tugging down on my eyelids. Mrs. Kinnington glared back at me but with tears in her eyes. She was trying to stand up.

"I think I know what's best for my grandson."

"So did the judge," I mumbled, at which point I sensed the polar bears come bustling back into the room.

Thirtieth

THE summer rain in Boston is somehow dry. It's made of water and falls from the sky in the usual way, but it never soaks you through. It's more like a refreshing breeze that clears the mugginess from the air.

"Funny, they take the carnations but leave the roses." I lifted the withered, crackly flowers and replaced them with fresh roses, yellow this time. I had to work with only one hand and slowly; my left arm was still in a tight sling, and the rib wouldn't hear of quick movements. I'd dragged a light folding beach chair down the path with me. I set it up with the help of my right foot. I eased into it, the light rain blowing on my face.

"Yep," I said, imitating an old man's voice. "Sure is good to rest the weary bones." Off to the left I noticed the elderly man again. He still wore the old gray suit, no raincoat, and held the Homburg. He was straightening back up with difficulty after laying some flowers near his headstone. I dropped the imitation from my voice.

"Suicide, Beth," I said, a little thickly. "Remember how we would talk around it, the last few weeks? When I wouldn't leave you alone. Well, they left him alone. Two days after Brower's—he's the DA—two days after his third psychiatrist agreed that Stephen couldn't stand trial, the kid tore open a pillow and shoved the stuffing down his throat. Kept shoving it till he choked. Mrs. Kinnington had just arrived at the hospital to visit him, special arrangements and all despite his, ah, status. The DA told me she saw him being rushed to a resuscitator. She had another stroke. The DA said he doubts she'll last the week."

The tissue paper around the roses was beginning to flatten here and bulge there from the rain. We watched the power launches and a few maverick sailboats slap against the light storm chop in the harbor below. And we talked. It was my first day back in quite a while, so we had a lot to catch up on.

After a time, I found myself watching the elderly man. He was still standing over his place, the Homburg clenched in his hands and his head bowed. His shoulders were shaking now, though, and every once in a while his torso would heave up, and he'd rock forward a little.

I decided it was time to go, before the weather started getting to me, too.